I0619550

CRIMES, CONSPIRACY, AND COURTSHIP

PADDY'S PEELERS MYSTERY
BOOK ONE

AUBREY WYNNE

PLATO PUBLISHING

Copyright © 2025 by Aubrey Wynne

All rights reserved.

No part of this book may be reproduced in any form or by any electronic or
mechanical means, including information storage and retrieval systems,
without written permission from the author, except for the use of brief
quotations in a book review.

ISBN: 978-1-946560-37-7

Edited by The Editing Hall

Logo Design by Sweet N' Spicy Designs

❀ Created with Vellum

SERIES LIST

Paddy's Peelers Mystery (Historical Romantic Suspense)
Sweet romance,
Crimes, Conspiracies, and Courtship
Pads, Purses, and Plum Pudding
Poisons, Potions, and Parasols

Once Upon a Widow (sweet Regency)
Earl of Sunderland
A Wicked Earl's Widow
Rhapsody and Rebellion
Earl of Darby
Earl of Brecken
Earl of Griffith
Beware a Wallflower's Wrath
A Wallflower's Wassail Punch
A Scoundrel's Christmas Challenge
The Duplicate Duke
Kiss the Scoundrel Farewell

PREFACE OF THE UNDERWORLD

The Oxford English Dictionary defines *underworld* as: 1. Sublunary or terrestrial world. 4.a. A sphere or region lying or considered to lie below the ordinary one. Hence also (figurative) a lower, or the lowest, stratum of society 4.b. The world of criminal or of organized crime (usually with the); hence, the inhabitants of this region.

This was the world of Paddy's Peelers.

* * *

"For alongside the world of Pride and Prejudice and the Nature poets there existed a pulsating, undisciplined urban underworld of young thieves, body-snatchers and gamblers. Pleasure-seekers and criminals alike were enjoying a final fling before the coming of the Metropolitan Police in 1829. Gambling and drinking were endemic in upper- and lower-class society, fraud in the middle classes."

Donald A Low *The Regency Underworld*

INTRODUCTION TO THE PEELERS

The Story of Paddy's Peelers

peeler, n. 1816
   ...Originally: a member of the Irish constabulary. Later: (more gen.) a police officer; spec. a member of the original London Metropolitan force...

Patrick O'Brien, previously of the Dublin Police Force, left Ireland with his wife Margaret and arrived in London in 1798. Paddy was frustrated with the lack of government involvement in crime and the poor, and the unreliable pay received by officers. He wanted to belong to an organized body of policing.

Margaret's stepbrother worked as a Bow Street Runner, and this new policing force greatly interested O'Brien. It was directly attached to the magistrates and court, housed at 4 Bow Street, and received some funds from the central government through grants. The Runners were to become the model of the future, proving to the government and the public that a professional police force could reduce crime.

O'Brien soon gained a reputation at the Bow Street court for his clever and expedient investigations. While his professional life provided him a great satisfaction, his personal life was lacking. Paddy and his wife lamented the absence of children in their household.

When Paddy stumbled across a sick waif in an alley of Seven Dials, he brought the lad home. Over the next ten years, their "family" grew to a brood of seven. The couple developed the unique talents of their six boys and one girl. As the children grew into adulthood, O'Brien created an investigative service utilizing the skills of his brood. All the men spent an allotted time as a constable for Bow Street, learning the trade from seasoned Runners while working in the "family business."

Nicknamed Paddy's Peelers (*peeler*: slang for an Irish policeman), O'Brien's crew became an efficient team that included detectives, a physician who doubled as a coroner for autopsies, a solicitor who specialized in criminal law, a female master of disguise able to infiltrate any level of society, and a barrister who later joined their ranks to present certain cases pro bono in High Court.

PROLOGUE

November 1798
St. Giles Rookery, London

*H*arry scooped out the ashes from the kitchen hearth and dumped them into a bucket. He took it outside to the alley and spread it in a wide line along the edge of the opposite building, knowing the rain would eventually wash it away. Swiping at his nose with a ragged coat sleeve, he stifled a cough. If the doxies knew he was getting sick, they'd throw him out. Most would scoff at the idea of a brothel being a good home, but it was better than where he'd come from.

True, he had a shared bed at the orphanage instead of the floor by the hearth. But the caretakers had been quick with a stick or their hand, whether it was for disobedience or to soothe their own foul mood. The schoolmaster had been particularly cruel, only leaving marks beneath the children's drab clothing. But the brutish schoolmaster had not worried about visible marks when Harry had tried to stop him from paddling the new girl.

She'd been the same age as him, around six, but so thin a stiff breeze could have knocked her over. The girl had stuttered, then shut her mouth tightly, and refused to answer the man's question. The smell of fear had hung heavy in the classroom. The schoolmaster had bent the frail girl over a table and began his customary ten smacks on her backside. The silence in the room had only intensified the girl's whimpering. By the fifth *whack*, she'd let out the most pitiful scream, and Harry had reacted without thinking.

Putting his hand on the man's paddle, he had looked up defiantly at the tutor. His stomach had knotted as he realized he would now take the punishment for the girl. Her ten smacks and ten more for his impudence and disobedience. Harry hadn't been able to sit for a week without holding back tears.

He had vowed during those seven days that he would never take another beating willingly, even if it meant being cast out or worse. So when the thin, crow-faced mistress struck him with the back of her hand for dropping a bucket, Harry had lost all sense—and hit her back.

The horror on her face had been a short-lived satisfaction.

His grin had been the last straw.

That afternoon, three women in tight-fitting, low-cut dresses and painted faces came to visit, watching him as he worked scooping coal. He was used to the people who paid to look at the orphans, though he had never understood it.

"How strong is he?" asked the plump woman with the frizzy blonde hair. "Let me see him lift something."

Harry carried two buckets of water across the stone floor of the kitchen, and they bobbed their heads as if pleased. His muscles strained, pulling on his shoulders and sending a dull ache down his back. A heavy flowery scent seemed to float off the ladies.

"Can he start a fire?" the older woman asked. Her hair was dark but streaked with gray. "We need someone to tend to the hearth."

"Aye, he can," Crowface said with a smug smile.

"He's no' a bit puny." The older woman approached him and squeezed his arm. She tipped his chin and pulled down his lower lip, squinting at his teeth. "Can you run fast?"

Harry nodded.

"Good, I don't like waitin' when I send you out on an errand."

"How old is he?" the redheaded woman asked. "I don't want 'im too old, or he'll skip off afore I get my money out of 'im. But I ain't gonna be accused of abusing a babe."

"Nine and growing stronger," Crowface had answered. Harry had bit his lip, knowing to correct the mistress would earn him a slap on the head.

"I suppose he'll do," said the older woman. She handed the mistress a tiny pouch of coin.

"He's slow, if ye know what I mean, so I expect he'll be loyal." Crowface shoved Harry toward the ladies, hissing in his ear, "Ye're where ye belong now. Good riddance."

"Wha' about me belongings?" he asked, his dark eyes darting from the group of ladies to the hall door. Could he get past her to run and get his box?

"I want another set of clothes to go along with 'im," said his new owner. "And let the poor lad collect his things."

Harry nodded at her in thanks and dashed to the dormitory room where all the boys slept. He wouldn't miss this sterile white room with its rows of identical counterpanes. Running down the second aisle of beds, he skidded to a stop before a middle mattress and dove underneath to clutch the small wooden box with the name

WALTERS crudely carved into the top. He wouldn't be able to say goodbye to any of his friends. Not that he had many.

When he returned to the kitchen, the women bundled him into a hackney coach, and the wheels lurched forward.

Away from the orphanage.

Away from the horrors of his childhood.

Away from the only home he'd ever known.

* * *

HE SOON LEARNED his new lodging was a house of prostitution. Harry was in charge of the kitchen fire, being instructed to keep it going all night long. Visitors often asked for meals during their nightly—or hourly—stays. The women also gave him daily errands to run, and when he finished his work, he was free to find more odd jobs to earn his own coin for clothing and entertainment.

He had a roof over his head and a thick blanket on the floor near the fire that he only shared with a few bedbugs. He had enough to eat. Other than an occasional smack if he got too impudent, he was left alone. After two years, he'd come to a conclusion.

Life was better with the ladybirds.

He mopped his forehead with a rough woolen sleeve, trying to wipe away the growing fever. There was a new abbess in charge, and she hated any kind of sickness, terrified even a mumbling of an affliction would chase away customers. Or worse, she might contract a disease. Harry knew he had to hide his condition and continue his duties, or she'd toss him in the alley. She'd done it to one of the "boarders" last month.

But two days later, he woke to a foot kicking him in the side.

"Wake up, ye lazy swine." A shadowy form hovered above

him, and he squinted. The voice reached down and touched his face. "Gordon! Come fetch this lad and get him out of here."

"Where ye want me to take him?"

"The workhouse for all I care. His face is as white as haddock's belly, and he's sweatin' like a horse after a long race. He ain't good for business, so he can't stay here."

Harry vaguely realized he was being carried. How could his skin be so hot, yet he felt so cold? He thought the bouncer was speaking to him, but then he was sitting on the cold ground, the smell of urine and rotting garbage filling his nostrils. Gordon pushed something under Harry's coat. *His box.*

Harry leaned his back against a hard stone wall. It was so cool against his skin, and he fell into a feverish sleep.

His dreams were vivid and frightening. The schoolmaster was chasing him, throwing pencils at him like knives. He jerked at the prickling sensation, wondering if he was bleeding. Then he was in the Thames, the muddy water rising about him. He splashed at the water, trying to reach the shore, but his legs were numb from the frigid river.

So cold. So tired. If he just rested for a while…

Harry woke in a groggy state, hands pulling at him, voices yelling and cursing him to move, get up. He felt the blow on his cheek, a pressure against his cheekbone, but not any pain.

Maybe he was already dead. But he was still cold. A person couldn't be cold in heaven.

Hands pulled at his coat, and his brain began to churn. *His box.* They were trying to steal his box. With his arms tight around his middle, he ducked his head. They would have to kill him first.

A roar brought him fully awake. Several boys were above him, trying to steal his coat and boots. Harry kicked at them in a panic. The booming growl sounded again. The boys looked up, their eyes wide, then ran. A giant's shadow covered him now, so he shut his eyes, waiting for the end.

But Goliath picked him up and wrapped him in something. It was heavy and so warm. Harry snuggled against the soft wool, sniffled, and sighed.

"I've got ye, boyo," said a deep, rumbling voice, "and ye're safe now. Let's just hope my Maggie t'inks dis is a grand surprise and not a terrible idea."

CHAPTER 1

Late September 1819
Covent Garden, London

*H*arry Walters whistled an old sailor's tune as he leaned against the damp brick wall. He had claimed a better-smelling alley than the last one. Odd, being it was a seedier part of Town, on the outskirts of Covent Garden. A rustling to his left sent a side-glance in that direction. A large rat peeked around a barrel, his whiskers trembling as he sniffed the air, black orbs darting back and forth. Their eyes met, and the rodent scurried away.

"Intelligent little vermin," Walters mumbled and returned his attention to the gaming hell across the street. The moon was hazy in the thick fog, casting irregular shadows up and down the street. There wasn't as much traffic tonight. The *clip clop* of horses pulling hackneys for hire echoed on the slick cobblestones. Pedestrians had dwindled as the hours passed.

He was a man of patience—had to be in his profession. Walters had been following the Duke of Colvin for three months now and had come to know him, in a sense. His Grace went to White's or one of the gentlemen's clubs two nights a week to keep up appearances with his peers. Three nights a week he wandered Vauxhall Pleasure Gardens or went to the theatre in Covent Garden.

Walters did his surveillance on these three nights, watching the duke arrive in his shiny black landau and blazing emblem, drawn by a team of sleek black horses. If he went to a play and had a woman accompanying him, it would be a short night for Walters. If the duke was alone, he would emerge from the theater, walk toward his coach, but duck into a hackney waiting just behind it. Then Walters knew the night was just beginning as he followed Colvin into the rougher parts of Covent Garden. The duke enjoyed gambling and doxies away from the eyes of the *ton*.

It was the same routine for Vauxhall, arriving in his own conveyance but leaving in another. Whenever Colvin was alone, he was looking to satisfy his baser desires. Since the duke's father had died six months ago, Colvin's tastes had become more and more vulgar. The reins restraining him had been cut, and he had moved from well-known "nunneries" to businesses willing to look the other way at some of His Grace's pastimes.

A woman and boy ambled up the street toward Walters, and he dipped his head, letting his cap shadow his face. He pulled the collar of his wool coat up, warding off the chilly fog as it threatened to envelop the city. As the pair approached, the woman halted in front of him, a gap showing in her broad smile.

"Ho there, 'andsome," she crooned. "Ye're looking lonely this fine night."

He shook his head. "Thank you for asking, ma'am, but I'm waiting for someone."

"Ye don't need to wait anymore, lover." She peered into his face and poked his linen shirt, hooking a finger in the material to pull him closer.

A strong odor of gin washed over him.

"Who ye waitin' fer? I can beat her price and show ye a better time." She pushed some stray frizzy hair back under her cap and winked at him.

He shook his head, reached down without looking, and snatched the boy's hand hovering above Harry's pocket. "I believe you're a bit too friendly, boyo." He gave a tight grin as he clasped the lad's thin wrist. "If you were a few years older, I'd snap this fragile bone. But since I'm in a fine spirit, I suggest you move on before the situation gets ugly."

The pair moved on, the boy scurrying while the woman threw an insult over her shoulder. Harry snorted and shook his head just as a hackney pulled up to the back of the gaming hell. The duke emerged, seeming irritated, slapping his gloves against one palm before entering the vehicle.

Who put a pin under his saddle? he wondered as he crossed the street and ambled toward the hackney. Walters was surprised when he heard the duke bark his home address. *Must have lost quite a sum.*

As he emerged from the side street, hailing his own ride home, he checked the time. Barely midnight. What had Colvin's hackles up to make him leave so early?

The hackney eventually made its way to Cheapside, turning onto Gracechurch Street. He paid the driver, then took the stairs to the front door of his home—the only real home he'd ever known—his mind on this latest case. It was usually quiet this time of night, so it surprised him to hear the sound of muffled laughter coming from the parlor.

He stopped outside the partially open door and only

heard more chuckling. All sounded well, he thought, as he took the stairs.

"Harry!"

Walters stopped, looking over his shoulder as Paddy O'Brien's head stuck through the doorway. "Come in and join us, boyo. We've got business to discuss."

"Now? It's after midnight."

"Thank ye fer da time, but last I checked, ye were no night watchman." The Irishman waved him into the room. "An old friend o' mine is here. An old friend from the *Home Office*."

Those last two words were enough explanation.

Walters followed Paddy into the parlor, nodding to Lord Chester Hatford. "My lord, it's a pleasure to see you again."

It was a cozy room, with a dark-green Wilton carpet spread before the hearth, a tinder box on the mantel, along with small frames of the O'Brien clan. The clan Paddy proudly called his family to anyone who cared to listen. He and Margaret O'Brien had collected seven misfits throughout their lifetimes, educating them, sending each in the direction best fitting their personalities and talents.

Maggie had mandated they all posed for a miniature at sixteen, then added it to the mantel collection. The matriarch and patriarch were in the center. The others were arranged by age rather than when they were found, alternately on each side, starting with Harry, Gus, Sampson, Clayton, Benjamin, Elijah, and Honora.

Each child was now a successful adult, living their own life, as well as being vital components of the O'Brien Investigative Services. The agency had been nicknamed Paddy's Peelers by the Bow Street Runners they worked with. Paddy being Patrick O'Brien's nickname, and the Peelers being the moniker given to constables and their men in Ireland.

Lord Chester interrupted his musings. "O'Brien has some of the best whiskey in Town. Have a glass with us."

Paddy handed Harry a glass of amber liquid and nodded toward a chair across from Hatford by the fire. The guest leaned forward, his silver hair still showing streaks of auburn. His broad shoulders and trim body belied his sixty years.

"Hatford has a tale I t'ought ye'd find interesting." Paddy threw back the rest of his Irish whiskey and poured another, standing by Harry, his forearm resting on the top of the leather chair. His Irish wolfhound, Aonarach, moved from the hearth to sit beside Paddy, his great tail thumping against the stone. The gray wire-haired beast was a mammoth of a dog and never left his master's side unless told to.

"No offense, my lord," began Walters, "but it never seems to bode well when we meet up in the wee hours of the night."

Hatford snorted. "You aren't wrong. I've explained the situation to O'Brien, and he's suggested you are my man. Have you had any dealings with the Spencean Philanthropists?"

Harry whistled. They were a radical group who had tried to overthrow the government several years back. The Home Office had planted a spy, stopped the plot, and arrested the men. Unfortunately, the spy was considered unreliable due to his past, and without better testimony, the cases had been dropped. "What are they up to now?"

"I'm afraid more of the same. Arthur Thistlewood is the leader now, and he's out for blood. Thinks force is the only way to be heard. We've been trying to find out what they're planning." Hatford sipped his whisky. "I've been on the case for the last two months."

"Do you have someone in place?" asked Walters.

"Yes, a fellow named George Edwards. Do you know him?"

Walters nodded. "He makes statues, doesn't he? Last I heard, he was in Windsor with a small shop."

"That's how we found him. Major-General Sir Herbert Taylor commissioned a sculpture from him and ended up recruiting him."

"I never considered him in the role of spy," Walters mused.

"Who knows what goes on in a man's head," added Paddy, then tipped his head toward Harry. "His own family could pass him by on the street when he's in disguise and never recognize him. A grand magician o' appearance, he is."

It was true. Walters prided himself on the ability to alter his appearance. There were times it was better he wasn't recognized—for him and those he loved.

"I trust Edwards. He's been accepted by Thistlewood and is gaining recognition within the group. Even began recruiting a few members himself for credibility."

"So why do you need me?" Walters was curious now. He had helped on several cases with the Home Office and was more than happy to do whatever he could to support the Crown.

"While Edwards has been worming his way into the Spenceans, I've been tracking their finances." Hatford grinned. "It seems we've been following the same wretched duke."

Walters rarely showed surprise, but this news almost dropped his jaw. "The Duke of Colvin is giving money to radicals?"

Hatford nodded. "I believe someone is blackmailing him. Rumor at White's was his father was a cheat in cards—"

"My client's father, the late Earl of Darby, lost a huge amount to the late duke in a sham of a game. Now he wants retribution for that and the present duke's... misdeeds."

"Well, it seems the son has been charged with the same offense as the father. To avoid scandal, he agreed to stay clear of White's. However, the proprietor did whisper in the ears of other club owners. He's been discreetly banned from the tables in any respectable place in London."

"That's why he's been moving into the less reputable gaming hells," murmured Walters. "He lives like a king but relies on the tables to keep him afloat."

"Colvin's never been politically active, taking his seat in the Lords for important votes. I asked myself, why would he support the Philanthropists and risk high treason?"

"Either someone knows more of his dark side than cheating at cards, or they've promised to restore him to the tables at the clubs." So Walters wasn't the only one following the duke. "How does he transfer the blunt?"

"He's been dropping off a payment at a coffee house in Cheapside. The first Tuesday of every month, Colvin arrives at five o'clock, orders a cup of coffee, and sits by himself while he drinks it. Within fifteen minutes, he drops a coin on the table and walks out." Hatford leaned forward again, pinning Walters with a grim stare. "He leaves the coffeehouse, pulls out a small leather pouch from under his waistcoat, and drops it at the corner of the building, in the alley."

"And?" Interesting this happened during the day *and* on one of Walters's off days.

"A boy pops out from the shadows and snatches it. Been going on for several months now."

This was an odd turn of events. *Was* he being blackmailed for his weekly forays into the dark back rooms of gin houses? Did someone else know of Colvin's slide into depravity? And if so, who? Walters drummed his fingers on the arm of the chair. His client, the Earl of Darby, was keen to bring this man to justice for other past—and personal—wrongdoings. If they could arrest Colvin for treason, it would be a boon for everyone. Except the duke, of course.

Paddy rubbed his jaw, the scratch of a day-old growth

breaking the silence. "I wouldn't mind seeing dat despicable arse in the Tower."

"Better yet, a noose around his neck," added Walters. He turned back to Hatford. "Again, why do you need me?"

"Two reasons. I need to know what Colvin is doing when he makes his social calls outside of polite society. We need something solid in order to question him, let alone arrest him, because he's a peer." Hatford fixed his tired brown eyes on Paddy. "It irks me how he can hide behind a title."

"If anyone can trap da devil, it's my Harry." He gave the man in question a hearty slap on the back, which caught Aonarach's attention. He gave the room a short, deep *ruff*. Paddy reached down the scratch the hound's ears.

"And the second reason?" Walters asked, wincing at the sudden assault by Paddy.

"I need someone to keep an eye on Edwards. I'm afraid he'll get in too deep and find himself in trouble." Hatford finished his drink and set the glass on the side table with a *thunk*. "Of course, we might also need one of the Peelers to testify if we are able to make a case."

Walters snorted. "Me?"

"I know you left Bow Street due to unwarranted accusations but later vindicated. I also know it was after you found incriminating evidence in a case that led to the higher echelons of society." Lord Chester paused as if embarrassed. "Considering your history... Well, we wouldn't want a repeat of the trial a few years ago. No insult intended."

Walters nodded. "Of course, and none taken." He stood and reached out his hand to shake Hatford's. "I'm happy to do my duty, Lord Chester. Just let me know when and where to start."

"How about now?" asked Hatford with a grin.

CHAPTER 2

Hanover Square, London

"*M*atilda Bancroft, are you listening to me?" Her mother's voice rose with irritation.

"Yes, Mama," Lady Matilda's eyes focused on the old man across the street with a bag slung over his shoulder. Was he collecting or selling something? It was the second time she'd seen him, and it was always when her brother was away on business. The first time, if she was correct it was the same man, had been in the dead of night behind the house. She hadn't been able to sleep and got up to look out the window. She'd seen him walking past the mews. "I should go out more. Put the books away and socialize with people my own age," she answered her mother.

"What are you looking at?" Lady Darby demanded.

"Nothing," Mattie lied, turning back to her mother. "I promise I will make an effort." But her thoughts remained on the old man.

He was an odd fellow—looking older than her mother yet toting a bag that looked heavy. She remembered the old worn coat because it had a rip near the collar. Or it at least appeared to from a distance. It could be a dismal attempt at darning. What was he doing in this neighborhood? Today, she thought their eyes had met, sending a shiver down her spine. Excitement or foreboding?

Now you're just being melodramatic.

"The Carstons are having a musicale this week. Perhaps we'll attend."

"Yes, Mama," Mattie murmured, moving away from the window and settling in front of the library hearth. It was a large room with dark paneling and overstuffed chairs clustered for groups of guests. An intricately embroidered chaise longue sat near the window, heavy drapes pulled back to let in the sunlight. The Axminster carpet was thick and plush beneath her slippers.

She waited to open a book, considering her mother's recent warning. "I heard there will be a violinist. It sounds lovely."

Her mother frowned at the unexpected compliance, then let out a breath. The expression on Lady Darby's face went from subtle annoyance to satisfaction. "Very well. Your brother sent word he shall be home by the week's end."

Mattie already knew that, but she wouldn't hurt her mother's feelings by telling her Nicholas had written to her. Even if the woman did harangue her about the upcoming Season. Mattie watched her leave, the perfectly tailored skirts *swishing* out the door, the flawless coiffure disappearing down the hall.

And then there was silence. Beautiful, serene, soul-healing silence.

She took in a deep breath and laid her head back against

the velvet-covered chair. The musicale would be another humiliating afternoon of being introduced to eligible men, of stuttering responses or falling silent too soon, and ultimately disappointing her mother.

Well, it could not be helped. Mattie was fortunate to have Nicholas as her older brother. He had made it clear to her that she could choose her husband—or not choose one at all —and he would deal with their mother.

"You only need to find the right man," Nicholas said, running a hand through his thick blonde hair. "Then the conversation will happen without force. You will know when you meet him."

"How does the interminable bachelor know such things?" she asked with a grin.

"Widower," he reminded her, his smile fading. "I know because you are the loveliest, cleverest, kindest woman in this miserable society. Any man who can't see that is an imbecile. And I won't have my sister shackled to an imbecile for the rest of her life."

"What if I don't find love, Nicky?" Yes, she was painfully shy, but once she came to know someone, the insecurity fled. But no one seemed to find her interesting enough to spend the time to find out.

"Then you'll be stuck with me for eternity." He kissed the top of her head, the same color as his, and snipped her nose. "He's out there. You are destined for love, my sweet sister. At nineteen, you have plenty of time to find him."

Well, in the meantime, she would try to please Lady Darby. It was the least she could do as a loving daughter. Who knows? Love might leap from behind a potted plant at Almack's and hit her over the head.

Mattie strolled along the shelves, looking for a good

novel. With all these thoughts of romance, she might as well read one. Her eyes strayed to the window, and she saw the old peddler was gone. She decided to ask their driver about him. Mr. Jones seemed to know everyone and their business.

* * *

THE NEXT DAY, Mattie waited at the portico for Mr. Jones to come around with the curricle. It was a lovely day, and she wanted to sketch. She wore her favorite pale-blue day dress that Nicholas said matched her eyes. A simple fine muslin with puffed sleeves and a square neck, it had tiny deep-blue birds embroidered along the sleeves and hem. A row of the same, but in white, had been sewn into the center of the midnight-blue satin ribbon around the high waist. She finished the outfit with a swooping, light-blue bonnet adorned with indigo lace and matching ribbons tied beneath her chin.

As the conveyance stopped in front of her, the driver hopped down and helped her up. Her maid, Franny Tilbot, came running out to join them.

"Your parasol, my lady," the maid said with a scolding look. "You mustn't burn your ivory skin."

Mattie rolled her eyes but took the parasol. Franny accepted the driver's help and joined her mistress, careful not to step on the leather bag stored on the floorboard with sketching materials. "I can hear the Lady Darby now, berating me for letting you come home with pink cheeks."

A touch of regret rolled through Mattie, realizing her maid may have received a tongue lashing because of her thoughtlessness. "I didn't think of it. I'm so glad I have you to keep track of all Mama's rules and worries. I would never subject you to one of her tirades if I could help it."

"Of course not," said the older woman, holding her cap on her auburn hair as the curricle lurched forward.

"Where to, m'lady?" Mr. Jones asked, tipping his black hat to reveal thick brown curls. His brow glinted with a slight sheen over the hazel eyes. "Hyde Park?"

She shook her head. "It's too late in the day. Too many people Mother knows will be there. Let's go to St. James's. I'll sketch the swans."

As Mr. Jones expertly weaved the curricle through the traffic, they passed St. George's and left Hanover Square. The traffic grew more congested the closer they came to St. James's. Mattie watched the passersby on the street as she twirled her parasol above her head. The curricle turned onto Cocksure Lane and soon Farrance's pastry shop came into view.

"Oh, Mr. Jones. Could we stop for an ice?" she asked, dabbing a handkerchief around her neck. It was abnormally warm for September.

"Yes, m'lady. It's a hot one for sure." He clicked to the horses and guided them to the side of the street, then helped both women down and across the street. "I'll wait here and guard the horses and the parasol," he said with a wink at the maid before settling his lean form against the stone wall of the sweet shop and pulling his hat low over his eyes against the bright sun.

Inside, customers sat at tables, eating dainty cakes and candied fruits, or spooning cold ices onto their tongue.

She and Franny took a seat at an empty table and a waiter soon came to take their order. "We'd like some ices to take to the park with us," she told him. "We'll be sure to return the dishes and spoons."

"Of course, ma'am," the young man said with a smile. "We have a special flavor today, our coffee ice."

"Ooh, I'll take one of those"—she turned to Franny—"for Mr. Jones, he loves his coffee. And I would like pistachio." She turned back to her maid with an arched brow.

"Oh, cherry, please, if you don't mind. But it's not necessary, Lady Matilda."

"Pishposh. The sun is just as hot on your head as it is on mine."

"If you'd like, I can bring this to you at the park," the young man said, obviously hoping for a tip.

"That would be lovely." She gave the man enough coin for four instead of three ices, which he accepted with a grateful smile and low bow. "We shall wait for you at The Mall entrance."

They went outside, and Mr. Jones escorted them along Spring Garden toward The Mall. Once he found the ladies a shaded spot, he left the satchel with Lady Matilda's sketching materials and returned to the carriage to check the horses.

St. James's was busy this afternoon. Couples strolled the mall lane, nannies chased their wards, and the swans and geese strutted with their families waddling behind. Mattie loved the mute swans. As a child, her father had brought her and Nicholas here several times to see the foot-guard parade. There was always a full band accompanying the changing of the guards, and she and her brother always enjoyed the show.

"Here he comes," said Franny as the waiter from Farrance's approached with a tray and three glass dishes with silver spoons. Right behind him trotted Mr. Jones.

The threesome strolled along a shaded lane and savored the icy sweet. Mr. Jones and Franny followed just behind Mattie, making pleased noises over their mistress's treat. When they finished, Mr. Jones made sure they were settled near enough to the lake and Duck Island for Lady Matilda to sketch the swans, then he returned the dishes to Farrance's.

"Oh, miss, it's a lovely day. Thank goodness for the breeze."

Mattie nodded. "If I enjoyed swimming, I'd be tempted to dip into the lake—except I don't think the swans would appreciate the intrusion."

"No, miss," agreed the maid with a chuckle. "My brother was bit by one when we were younger. Right in the nose. It swelled up like a loaf of bread on the rise."

"Oh, my. Did it hurt much?"

Franny nodded. "For a week or so. My mother said he was lucky it was his nose and not his eye."

The next hour, Mattie sketched a pair of white mute swans and their three cygnets, smiling at the little ones waddling behind their parents. She looked down at her drawing, considering the colors she would use when she painted it.

A scream pierced the quiet afternoon. Mattie and Franny looked about but only saw a toddler on their right. He wobbled toward the lake as fast as his short chubby legs could carry him, yelling "Wanny, wanny!" His goal seemed to be the baby swans, his arms held wide and a huge smile on his face.

"He's headed for the water," cried Mattie, looking about to see if Mr. Jones was watching. But the driver was a good distance away, talking with another man.

She didn't know how to swim, so Mattie knew she had to intercept the boy before he reached the lake. As she pushed the sketchbook from her lap, a blur of white and dark blue streamed past her on the left, heading in the same direction as the redheaded toddler. The man dropped his black coat as he ran pell-mell for the pending disaster.

One of the adult swans stepped in front of the cygnets with a loud snort and moved toward the child, its wings half spread, its neck curved back in an aggressive stance. An attack by such a large creature upon the much smaller one could create serious injury. With lightning speed, the swan jabbed its beak at the boy just as the man swooped between them.

He grabbed the child as he fell onto the ground and rolled, tucking the boy against his chest. Another streak, this time a jonquil day dress and the same red hair, flew across the lawn and snatched the toddler from the man as he rose from the ground. She began thanking the dark-haired gentleman, when both adult swans rushed toward the trio, hissing ferociously. The mother backed away, then ran, the babe's wail drowned out by the raspy honks of the swans. The poor hero backed away from the angry parents, hands out to protect himself, as one of the birds began making an atrocious hoarse, trumpet-like sound.

The swans continued their berating as the man grew closer and closer to the lake. Mattie put a hand over her mouth and looked at Franny. Both women's eyes were wide. "He doesn't understand they are growing angrier because he's moving in the wrong direction."

"He needs to move away from the water and the cygnets," agreed the maid.

Mattie jumped into action. She grabbed her parasol and ran toward the lake. "Come toward me," she yelled at the reluctant hero.

The gentleman looked up at her just when a swan reached out with its bill and caught his hand. As the man shook his hand away from the bird, he lost his balance, arms flailing wide, and fell into the water.

Mattie made it to the shore as the adult birds were about to pursue their quarry into the pond. She chased them back with her parasol, opening it as she shooed them. It gave their victim enough time to rise from the pond, water sluicing off him. By this time, the cygnets had swam farther down the shore, and the parents turned and followed their brood into the water.

"Oh dear," Mattie began, then assessed the man coming toward her. He was handsome, medium height and strongly built, the wet linen shirt clinging to the muscles of his arms. "Oh dear," she sputtered again.

CHAPTER 3

"Are you hurt?" he asked, dark chocolate eyes pinning her with an intense stare.

"Me?" She shook her head. "No, but your hand is bleeding. Come, let's get your coat and take a look at that bite."

He ran a large hand through his dripping brown hair. "I'm fine, but I thank you."

"Nonsense." Her tone brooked no argument. "You can dry in the sun while I bandage your hand with... something."

He followed her back to Franny and Mr. Jones, who had come running during the commotion.

"Well done, sir," said Mr. Jones with a grin. "The lad would have had a battle scar to show for that if you hadn't intervened."

"You're a hero," said Mattie as they settled on the grass. She dug through her satchel and found the cloth she used to wipe her hands. "I don't have anything to wet it with."

"And no one's going near the water again," added Franny. "I've heard those mute swans can kill a person."

"An exaggeration, I'm sure." Mattie shook her head. "But they can definitely do harm. Now, let's see that hand."

She kept her gaze down, not trusting herself to look in the man's eyes again. The fluttering in her stomach had just quieted. But she wasn't prepared for the touch of his skin against hers. Warm and rough and… tingly.

No, his fingers weren't tingling, she was. Sucking in a breath, she turned his hand to inspect the bleeding. The bite had torn the piece of skin between the thumb and forefinger. She dabbed at the blood, wondering how long it would take for someone to fetch water.

"I have something to pour over it, Lady Matilda," said Mr. Jones, handing her a small silver flask.

She looked up at her driver, one brow arched as she took liquor.

"And before you ask, I do not partake while working. It's for emergency use, such as we have right now."

Mattie grinned, then turned back to the injured hero. "This will hurt," she warned, holding the flask over the bite.

"Can't be any worse than the swan." The timbre of his voice was deep yet soft, setting the wings to flight in her belly again. "I'll try not to cry."

She let out a loud, happy guffaw that silenced the fluttering. "Oh," she squeaked, embarrassed at the volume of her laughter. But his jest had put her at ease. Pouring some of the alcohol over the wound, she handed Mr. Jones back his flask. She quickly cleaned the small area where the skin had been torn, but with the blood gone, the injury appeared to be minor.

Mattie used one of her handkerchiefs to wrap his hand, then leaned back to inspect her handiwork. "I think you will live," she declared with a smile. "It looks as if you may have a bruise on your jaw soon. The skin isn't broken, but it's beginning to swell. It hit you with its wing when you grabbed the child." She pointed to the left side of his face above his soggy cravat.

"I hadn't even noticed." He rubbed at his jaw, then winced.

"A cool compress will help when you get home."

"My immense thanks, Lady Matilda…" His voice went up in question.

"Bancroft," she supplied. "I suppose introducing ourselves is necessary considering the circumstances. We've become rather close in the past quarter hour."

"Aye, my lady," he murmured, his gaze holding her captive.

Breathe, just breathe. "This is my lady's maid, Miss Tilbot, and our driver, Mr. Jones."

"I'm Mr. Harry Walters, at your service," he said, bowing his head, then nodding to the servants.

"Hello, Mr. Harry Walters. May I shorten it to just Mr. Walters?" she asked with a grin.

"Whatever you prefer. I answer to many names." He chuckled, then said, "Most women are put off by the sight of blood. I'm impressed by your fortitude."

"I volunteer in the children's ward of the hospital. Working with children, one must have a strong stomach."

And just like that, her shyness went into hiding. They talked for an hour as they lounged on the blanket, asking questions of one another or just making observations. The butterflies went to sleep, and Mattie felt as comfortable in conversation with this man as she did with her brother's friends. Not that he invited many to the house, but there were a few.

"I've always wondered why they call those birds mute swans. They certainly make noise," Mattie mused after a short silence. "I never realized they could be so intimidating."

"Coming from the woman who tried to beat them down with her parasol." He chuckled and winked at her. "You are the true heroine of the day."

"Pishposh. There isn't a courageous bone in my body."

Though she blushed, pleased with his compliment. He made her feel a bravado she was sure she didn't possess.

"There's mythology relating to the mute swan. Do you know it?" he asked.

"I'm a bluestocking, no mistake, but I've read mostly Roman mythology. I assume this is Greek?"

"It is. Would you like to hear it?"

"Oh yes." Did she gush? Oh my, how proud her mother would be.

"You've heard of Zeus, of course, and Apollo, who pulled the sun across the sky every day in his golden chariot?"

She nodded and smiled encouragingly.

"This tale is about Apollo's son, Phaeton. They were both chariot drivers, and Phaeton had just won a race. The prize, given by his father, was a gift of the winner's choosing. Before Phaeton decides on what to ask for, he gets into an argument with his friends on whether he was skilled enough to drive his father's golden chariot.

"So, Phaeton decides that is what he wants as his prize, knowing his father is a man of his word."

"Why are young men so often vain?" Mattie asked, trying not to sound smug, then laughing at herself. "I'm sorry, please go on."

"Phaeton manages the first half of the ride brilliantly. When he lets go of the reins to wave to his friends, proving how capable he is, the horses, with no guidance, head straight for the earth. Fortunately, Phaeton pulls them up before they crash, but the earth below them is scorched."

"I remember something about this... He created the Sahara Desert."

"Very good, Lady Matilda. The destruction continued. When the seas began to boil, Poseidon demanded Zeus stop the chaos. So, the god struck Phaeton from the chariot, sending him to his death but ending the devastation."

"Why do gods always kill first and think later?" she mused out loud.

Mr. Walters laughed. "Do you ask questions throughout the performance when you go to the theater?"

"Constantly. My mother hates attending with me. But what does this have to do with the mute swan?"

"Phaeton's best friend, young Cycgus, wailed over Phaeton's dead body. It tortured Apollo, and when he couldn't make the young man stop, he changed Cycgus into a mute swan. According to the myth, the swans will live their entire lives in silence until death. Then they wail one last time as they leave this earth."

"That's why they call the babies cygnets." Mattie thought about this. "Could you imagine being silent your entire life? How dreadful."

"I know several people I wish I could silence." He chuckled, and she noticed how the tiny bit of silver at his temples blended into those soft, thick waves of brown.

What would it feel like if she reached up and touched his hair? *Too many novels and adventurous heroines, young lady,* she scolded herself.

Mr. Walters stood, held out his hand, and helped her up. "I must be on my way," he said, bowing over her hand. He searched the ground, found his coat, and shook it out before placing it over his arm.

* * *

WALTERS WAS at sixes and sevens. Lady Matilda Bancroft was lovely and guileless. And his employer's sister. After seeing Colvin's coach drive by one night in early August, Darby had asked him to keep an eye on the townhouse whenever he was away on business. Usually he sent Elijah, the youngest member of the family. Eli was also working on Bow Street now as a Runner, a requirement mandated by O'Brien to learn the basics of an investigation.

Twice, Walters had taken a watch to ensure all was well. He would never assume to speak with Darby's sister or mother. Yet, here he was, completely by accident, enjoying the afternoon being doctored by the lovely Lady Matilda. *Mattie*, Darby called her. She looked more like a Mattie than a Matilda. Mattie was warmer, friendlier.

He noted the disappointment in her clear blue eyes. She had her brother's looks, but her eyes were a hazier, lighter blue. Like a summer's day through a piece of muslin. The kind of eyes that made a heart beat faster and a mouth go dry. The kind of eyes he could look at all day.

Steady, Harry. She's out of your reach.

"Will I see you again?" Her gaze left his face now, as if she already knew his reply.

"I doubt it, my lady. I rarely chase children or get pummeled by fowl." He hesitated, then added, "I'm sure we move in much different circles."

"She doesn't move in any circles," mumbled the older maid, then looked in the direction of the mall lane, finding the passersby immensely interesting.

Darby had spoken of his sister and her lack of enthusiasm for London society, though he'd said it with something akin to pride in his voice rather than disappointment or irritation.

"Again, my gratitude for your assistance—"

"You'll have to return my handkerchief," she blurted out, immediately turning an adorable pink.

Harry began to unwrap the handkerchief but her hand on his stopped him. He stared at her hand, felt the warmth of her skin rush through his own body.

"A gentleman would wash it before he returns it." She peeked up at him through her long pale lashes.

He blinked. "I-I… of course. Shall I return it—"

"Here, next week. Same time and place." Now her gaze met his, a pleading look.

He tried to say no. Opened his mouth, waited for the word to escape. It was a simple two-letter response. His tongue would not cooperate. His brain commanded, and his heart refused. *I'd rather face the fires of hell.*

"Well then, I'll see you next week." With that, she gave him a brilliant smile, which set him on fire, picked up her satchel, and walked away, leaving her maid and driver to gather the blanket and scurry to catch up.

He watched her petite figure sashay toward Spring Garden, that deuced parasol spinning circles above her head.

He knew instinctively she had no idea how seductive her walk was. No idea how beautiful she was. No idea the effect she had on a man. Well, this man, anyway.

He would return the handkerchief next week and not see her again. Harry Walters was an orphan from the rookery. He was not a magical creature from mythology who could bend the world—or the London *ton*—to change his humble beginnings. Even as he firmly told himself it didn't matter, his head turned against his will to get one last glimpse of Lady Matilda Bancroft.

CHAPTER 4

The next day
Gracechurch Street, Cheapside

*H*arry tried to hurry through his breakfast before anyone joined him. His left jaw was now a lovely bluish-purple, and his right hand still tender from the bite. Being right-handed, he hoped there would be no need to plant anyone a facer in the near future.

"What in heaven's name happened to ye?" asked Margaret O'Brien, shattering Harry's plan of escaping unseen. Her auburn hair, streaked with silver that she blamed on her brood of seven, was tucked into a white mobcap. She wore a simple pale-rose muslin day dress which fit snugly about her rounded hips.

With a sigh of resignation, he set down his fork and looked at the woman who had raised him. A quiet growl escaped when he saw Paddy right behind her. Nearing sixty, the Irishman still towered over most men, his body large and solid with fists like anvils. His face was creased from both laugh lines and years, and his red hair had faded, but he could still make a younger man quake if pushed.

"Seems our boyo has been in a wee scrape," his father said with a smirk. "Business or pleasure?"

"Neither."

"'Tis a shame, it is." Paddy moaned with a shake of his head. He sat down at the head of the table, Aonarach lying down next to him. "Did ye get jumped?"

Harry opened his mouth, then shut it. He couldn't tell them what really happened. He'd be ridiculed for years to come.

"He tangled with a swan at St. James's Park." Honora O'Brien, the only daughter—and the only child raised from infancy by the O'Briens—stood in the doorway, her glorious red curls spilling over her shoulders and down her back. "Guess who won?"

"You can wipe the grin off your face, Sister. And how did you come by that story?" Harry knew, of course, but needed a moment to explain the incident in the best light.

"You were with Jack when it happened," she said, meaning the stage manager of the theater where she was presently working. Nora Diamond, her stage name, was a vital part of the Peelers' team. As a female, she could play a barmaid or flower seller or damsel in distress and eavesdrop on conversations the men could never get close to. "He told me all the details."

"A bird got da best o' ye?" Paddy's ruddy face split with a husky guffaw. His blue eyes shone as he took stock of his eldest son. "Tell me it was a big one at least."

Harry tossed a glare over his shoulder at his sister, shoveling in the last of black pudding so he could get away before he lost what little dignity he had left. "Little saucepot," he mumbled.

Nora snorted, poured a cup of tea, and sat down next to him, squinting as she inspected his jaw. "Let me see the hand," she demanded, holding out her hand for his.

He moved his right hand across his chest to show her. She held his fingers, then poked at the bite.

"Ouch, what the devil are you doing?" Harry snatched his hand back, sending another glower at his amused sister.

"Just wanted to see if it hurt," Nora said innocently, her shoulders shaking with mirth. "Don't be such a hen."

Margaret pursed her lips, most likely to hide her own grin, and scolded her and her husband. "Da poor man is injured and ye ridicule him. I taught ye both better'n dat."

"Thanks, Maggie," Harry said with a smirk at Nora. Good lord, why did his sister bring out the boy in him with every argument? No matter, he loved them all.

"Correct me if I get anything wrong, dear Brother." Nora turned to her parents. "According to Jack, he met Harry at St. James's to give him some information on a patron. A woman screamed. Her boy had run off while she'd been speaking with a friend, and she panicked, not knowing where he was. Our dear Harry"—she paused to pat his bruised jaw—"saw the lad running for the lake and the mute swans. Knowing how vicious those creatures are, he took off running to intercept the toddler.

"He then proceeded to throw himself in front of the boy just as another swan joined the first in an attempt to peck the young boy to death."

"That's a bit dramatic, I think," interrupted Harry.

"I'm an actress," she reminded him. "Anyway, he did one of those athletic rolls, then popped up like he was on wagon springs—"

"I did no such thing. It makes me sound like some odd children's toy."

Nora ignored his protest and continued, "I'm just

repeating Jack's version. Anyway, the mother had come around by this time and relieved him of her child, but the swan still wanted vengeance against poor Harry." She pouted her lips and batted her eyes. "Now who will save the hero?"

Harry groaned, Maggie giggled, and Paddy slammed the flat of his hand on the table, rattling the teacups.

"Dis tale must get even better, boyo, for ye're turning as red as yer sister's hair." Paddy slammed the table again.

"This brave man continued to back away from the swans, not wanting any trouble, but not realizing he was moving in the direction of their precious cygnets. One reached out and grabbed his hand, making Harry lose his balance and fall into the lake."

"They didn't follow him in?" asked Maggie. "Da fowl don't usually give up so easily."

Harry pushed his plate away, crossed his forearms on the table, and hid his head in them.

"Oh, they would have but a courageous, wisp of a lady ran to his defense and fought them off with her parasol."

Oh the humiliation. Harry wanted to crawl under the table.

When Paddy finally took a breath, a tear leaking from his eye, he said, "We can't let dis get around, boyo. It'd be bad for business."

More laughter.

"Get yer head up, Son, and face it like a man. No hiding from things in dis family." Paddy stood and went to the sideboard to fill a plate. "I'd like to meet da lass who saved ye from da wicked fowl."

"That's the interesting part," added Nora, slipping the hound a bite of toast. "It seems he joined the young lady and her maid afterwards. The lady bandaged his hand."

"A savior and a nurse? What does she look like?" asked Maggie, a glint in her dark-brown eyes.

"Very pretty," admitted Harry.

"And her name?"

He shook his head.

"Ye didn't ask? Where were yer manners?" Maggie crossed her arms over her ample chest. "Or ye don't want to tell us?"

Paddy joined them, his plate piled with eggs, meat, pudding, and toast. "Ye know I can find out easy enough. Hard to keep a secret when ye're living with detectives."

"Lady Matilda Bancroft." Harry sipped his coffee and focused on the tablecloth, waiting for the thunder.

"Titled. Interesting…" mused Maggie.

"She's da *sister* of a client!" Bellowed Paddy. "Have ye lost yer bloody mind?"

"Language," scolded Maggie.

"She insisted on tending to my injury and allowing my clothes to dry in the sun. Her maid and driver were there, and nothing inappropriate happened."

"Does she know who ye are?" demanded Paddy.

"I couldn't very well give her a false name. But no," Harry said, "she doesn't know what I do for a living or that I'm on a case for her brother."

Paddy grunted. "Since ye won't be seeing her again, I suppose no harm's been done."

"I have to return her handkerchief."

"Have someone else do it," Paddy ordered around a mouthful of sausage. He pointed his fork at Harry. "We don't need da wrath of an earl upon us because ye're flirtin' with his sister."

"We were only talking," Harry said between gritted teeth.

"And now ye're done talking."

It irked Harry to be *told* what to do. He was nine and twenty, almost thirty. But Paddy was right, and Harry *had* attempted to walk away.

"Talk to him like a man, not da boy ye brought home," Margaret reminded her husband gently.

Paddy had the decency to look sheepish. "She's right. I know ye'll do da right t'ing, Harry. I t'ink I get a wee jealous sometimes because I can't join ye as much as I'd like now."

It was Harry's turn to be embarrassed. This couple had given him so much.

Life. He'd have been dead in that alley if Paddy hadn't found him. Maggie doctored him back to good health, then taught him to read and write. He'd been unable to learn at the orphanage, but Maggie's patience and gentle insistence he *could* learn had proved a magical combination.

While she had educated him with books, Paddy had taught him life skills: how to deal with people, the difference between right and wrong, how one's word made the man. Harry had been used to physical labor, but the O'Briens rewarded him for it, making him want to work even harder. Every night when he'd gone to bed, he'd pray, *If I do my best, better than my best, let me stay. Let them keep me.* Sure, the couple had said their home was his home now, but he knew all shelter came with a condition.

It took over a year to believe he was part of a family. He began to enjoy the attention they lavished on him. The kisses and hugs were uncomfortable at first, considering the only affection he'd witnessed had been between the doxies and the men who paid for it. He didn't dislike it; he had nothing to compare it to, no past experience to relate it to.

It took another year to return the tenderness shown to him. He had nightmares until he was twelve about waking up in a cold, damp alley to find Paddy and Maggie and his new life had only been a dream.

"I can't argue with the logic," acknowledged Harry, bringing his thoughts back to the conversation. "I agree, but I gave her my word I would return the handkerchief next week. I'll keep my word, and that will be the end of it."

Paddy gave a nod, smeared his toast with marmalade, and winked at his wife. "We raised him good, eh?"

"Indeed. We raised them all good." Maggie beamed at Nora and Harry. "And they've given back two-fold."

* * *

WALTERS HAD one last stop before he went home. It had been a long day, gleaning information about the Spenceans from sources the Home Office or the spy Edwards didn't have. Now he would meet Sampson at the Dog's Bone and see how another case was progressing, one close to his brother's heart.

The tavern was busy as always. It smelled of sweat, stale alcohol, fresh bread, and fish. The latter obviously was part of the ingredients bubbling in the giant kettle over the fire. To his left was a long wood counter, scuffed but highly polished, where a half dozen men leaned against it, drinking and arguing good-naturedly. The rest of the large room was filled with tables and booths, mostly occupied by neighborhood patrons. Bess, the barmaid, squeezed past him with several bumpers gripped in one hand, acknowledging him with a smile.

"Eating or just drinking?" she asked, pushing a stray brown lock back under her mobcap.

"Drinking, the usual, please." He returned her smile and waved to Leo, the barkeep and owner, who nodded toward the back room.

"It's already waiting for you," Bess threw over her shoulder as she disappeared into the crowd.

Sam must have already arrived. Walters moved past the brawny, bald man, murmuring a thank-you for generously offering the space for the Peelers to use when they needed privacy. He greeted several familiar faces with a grin or bob of his head.

Walters ducked under the original doorjamb and entered a small room that transported him back two hundred years. Shelves had been added to the stone walls, and overhead, the low charred timbers from years of smoke silently told how long this building had been a part of London. This was Leo's storeroom, doubling as his office.

In the center was a scarred table where Sampson sat studying a paper, a plate with bread and cheese in front of him. Leo's wife always made sure they had a "little something" when they were back here. The Peelers often met here to discuss progress on their present cases. The only "office" Paddy had was the parlor at the house. Cases were mostly referred by Bow Street or past clients, and appointments usually took place at the client's home or a neutral location. Maggie had put her foot down long ago, demanding at least a minimal separation of domestic and professional lives.

Walters had always thought it best not to have a particular address where someone could see potential clients come and go.

"Harry, it's good to see you," said Sam, standing and stretching out his hand. "I hated missing Sunday dinner, but I had an emergency."

CHAPTER 5

*D*r. Sampson Brooks was the second lad the O'Briens had taken in. His parents had been sent to debtor's prison after his father's bookstore had burned to the ground. The Brooks's had found out too late that the insurance they had purchased was a fraudulent policy.

"Who did you save and not charge this time?" asked Walters with a shake of his head.

"I always get paid, but it's often not in coin," argued Sam with a grin. He was tall and lean, with brown hair, hazel eyes, and dimples that the ladies seemed to love. "There was an accident in Seven Dials. A boarding house caught fire, and the roof caved in, so I spent the day and night tending to injuries. The good Lord must have been watching over them for no one died."

"You usually help closer to White Chapel or Spitalfields."

"It happened in the early hours when most everyone was sleeping. After the roof collapsed, the whole building fell like a house of cards. Some escaped, but we had to dig some out." Sam's jaw tightened. "I hate the rookeries. It's hard enough to survive each day without catastrophes like that."

Walters respected his brother. The O'Briens had seen the boy's interest in science and medicinal plants and provided him with an education. In return, Sampson gave back to the poor as best he could, acted as a coroner for the Peelers, and patched his brothers up when needed.

Since Dr. Brooks had wealthy clients who paid the bills, he allowed the rookery women to cook, clean, and sew for him in exchange for medical assistance. Men would provide whatever skills they had to offer or a complimentary pint when going to the right taverns.

"You're a good man, Brother," said Walters. "And I have some good news and bad news for you."

"Never a good statement. What's the good news?"

"By a stroke of luck, I have a lead on three of the men who were involved in the insurance fraud that ruined your father. Of course, they were minor players and have moved on to other things." Walters shrugged. "However, we will keep an eye on their movements and see what we can find."

"Harry, *you're* a good man to keep working on an old crime which has nothing to do with you." His tone hardened. "But if we can find any wrongdoing to pin on even one of them, I will attend the hanging—or watch them sail away if transported—and restore peace in my soul. It's a thorn that has poked me for far too long."

"You're my brother, so what concerns you, concerns me. You'll get retribution, Sam. I just can't say when." He finished his ale and stood, snatching a hunk of bread and cheese to take with him. "I'm hoping you won't be so old you need a cane to get to Newgate."

* * *

One week later

Mattie sat on the blanket, her sketch pad on her lap, but

her hand idle. She smiled at the mute swans, thinking back to Mr. Harry Walters in a wet linen shirt and sodden waistcoat clinging to his body. She gave her maid a sideways glance, her fingers over her lips to hide her smile. The man was so… so… masculine.

Usually, men like that would have sent her running for the nearest corner or plant to hide behind. Not Mr. Walters. After an initial stumble, her shyness had evaporated like dew beneath the hot morning sun. He was unlike any man she'd known—aside from family. Words had spilled from her mouth, and her usual habit of questioning had peeked out.

"Here he comes, my lady," Franny whispered loudly.

Mattie looked up and her breath caught. He wore another dark coat today, His hat covered his head, and a waistcoat of gray and white stripes could be seen beneath the dark coat. His gray trousers were so… snug. A warmth rushed through her.

"Stop staring and start sketching," scolded her maid with a chuckle. "You'll scare him off before you can ask."

"Do you think he'll go along with our plan?" Mattie chewed her bottom lip. She prayed he would agree.

"Good afternoon, Lady Matilda," he said, his shadow covering them as he peered down on her, then nodded toward the maid. "Ma'am."

"It is, isn't it?" Mattie willed her stomach to behave and hoped her hand didn't shake when she held it up to Mr. Walters. "Will you sit with us?"

He hesitated. "I apologize, but I don't have much time." He lowered himself onto the blanket. "An unexpected appointment…"

Mattie pushed back the disappointment. "Well, you're here now. Your jaw is no longer swollen. How is your hand?"

"Healed and in use again." He reached inside his coat and

retrieved her handkerchief, clean and neatly folded. "Once again, I thank you for your assistance. I owe you a favor."

They spoke of the mother and child and wondered what happened to them. Mattie wondered if the child had any lasting fears of the swans or if he had no idea there had ever been any danger.

"More questions, Lady Matilda. You have an inquisitive mind," he said.

"After our adventure, I decided to read more about swans in mythology. Do you know the story, *The Children of Lir*?" Mattie pressed her lips together, hoping this might keep him with her longer.

"No, I can't say I have. Tell me," he said, leaning back on his hands and stretching his muscular legs out.

She pulled her eyes from his lap and took a deep breath. "It's Celtic folklore about four siblings who are turned into swans. Their father was the sea god, Mir, and his people were known to be magical."

"Of course. Every good story must have magic, a hero, a victim, and a villain." He grinned. "Please, go on."

"Well, after Lir's wife died, he married her sister. She became jealous of her nieces and nephew, for they loved their father and dead mother more than her."

"This cannot end well."

Mattie giggled. "No, trouble is coming."

"Or there would be no tale to tell."

"So this wicked woman turned the children into swans. The spell would last nine hundred years."

"Definitely magic. I wonder if that is why swans are so testy," he mused.

She burst out laughing. "Perhaps. Anyway, they would spend three hundred years in three different lands, and the spell would not be broken until they heard a bell ring by the new god."

"And what did the mighty god Mir do when he learned his children had come across *fowl play?*" Mr. Walters wiggled his dark eyebrows, sticking out his neck and flapping his arms like great wings. "Too much?"

She held back another laugh and shook her head. "He banished her, declaring her to be a demon of the air. After nine hundred years, monks arrived. The children heard the church bells and appeared in their human form."

"Seems a satisfying ending. I find the Celtic tales are usually quite dark."

"Ah, there's more. Once human again, they aged rapidly and soon died." She sighed dramatically. "The poor star-crossed family."

"You would get along well with my sister," he said, giving her a smile that could cause apoplexy in the sternest of women. She resisted the urge to fan her warm cheeks.

"Why would you say that?"

"She's an actress, very dramatic, very talented."

"Perhaps I will meet her someday." She risked a glance at him from beneath her lashes.

He shook his head. "I doubt it, my lady. As I said before, we are worlds apart. And I must be going."

She put a hand on his arm as he started to rise. "Yet you feel so close."

"*Hmph*, yet so far away."

Was his tone almost sad? Or was it her imagination?

He stood this time and held out a hand to help her to her feet. When they were facing each other, he held her gaze. "I will never forget you, Lady Matilda Bancroft. I wish you happiness and good fortune." He bowed and turned on his heel.

"Wait!" Mattie called, her heart racing. She couldn't let this man walk out of her life. Not yet. "I will call in that favor."

He froze, his back straight. Slowly, he turned back to her, his brown eyes questioning.

The words poured from her as if she only had seconds to get her thoughts out. "I am to attend the next Season, and I fear it will be a disaster. I cannot seem to hold a conversation with a man. My shyness is like a boulder on my back, and I cannot shake it off."

She stopped for a breath.

"You have no trouble conversing with me," he said, narrowing his eyes. "And I don't attend balls or musicales or... what are they called... *crushes*."

"Exactly. I'd like to meet with you and practice... being with a man." She was amused to see this rugged man's neck turn dark red. Then she realized how her statement might have been taken, and it was her turn to pinken. "I mean, practice dialogue, become comfortable speaking with the opposite sex."

"I don't think this is a good idea. Your family—"

"Will never know. It will be our secret. We will decide on a meeting place and bump into each other." Panic was rising in her throat. "I am terrified of having a proper Season, standing with the wallflowers, not knowing what to say, and my mother glaring at me. Or worse, stuttering when I do try to speak."

He had opened his mouth to deny her, but his expression changed. He was softening.

"It is too much when we've only just become friends, isn't it?" Mattie blinked back tears, not sure if they were for the horrid Season she would endure or the thought of never seeing this wonderful, handsome man again.

To her surprise, he reached out and took her hand. Her bare hand because she was supposed to be sketching. His touch sizzled her skin; her breath hitched. What would his arms feel like, wrapped around her, holding her close? When her gaze met his, she thought the wings in her belly would lift her into the air. Those chocolate eyes set her adrift, floating, hoping.

"Why do you know it will be such a disaster?" he asked softly.

"Mama was ill last spring, then I sprained my ankle. By the time I entered society, the Season was almost over." She closed her eyes and shuddered. "It was the most dreadful month of my life. Please, say yes."

"How can I tell you no when tears are shining in those lovely blue eyes?" He squeezed his fingers, then dropped her hand with a sigh. "Though it's against my better judgment."

Her heart soared, and she beamed at him. "Thank you, Mr. Walters. Thank you. You don't know how much I appreciate this. I'm happy to pay you for your time."

Anger flashed in his eyes. Oh, no. She had insulted him. "I mean we could consider this a business arrangement if it makes you more comfortable. Please, I meant no offense."

He blew out a breath. "Of course not. None taken."

Relieved, Mattie smiled again and blinked away the hot tears. "Do you enjoy art? We could meet at the Royal Academy."

"I do and we shall. Name the day and time and I will be there."

CHAPTER 6

$\mathcal{M}$attie ran up the stairs to her bedchambers, threw open the door, and launched herself onto the canopied bed. He would meet her at the Royal Academy next week. She had already been to the summer exhibition, but there was so much to see. And talk about. To a man. A very handsome man.

"If you act with such wild abandon, your mother will know something is up," Franny warned, smoothing her own reddish-brown tresses back into place. "Will you be able to keep your word to Mr. Walters?"

Mattie chewed her bottom lip. "I will. I must. If I can practice the inane topics I'm not supposed to venture from during the Season, then Mama will be placated."

"From your expression at the park, and this moment, I have grave doubts." She paused, then blurted, "It would break my heart if someone broke yours."

Mattie's hand went to her chest. "Franny, what a beautiful sentiment." She ran to the woman who had been like an older sister and hugged her tightly. "I will be fine. I realize I am smitten with Mr. Walters because he's the first man I'm comfortable with. No illusions there. I think our plan will work."

"What plan?" asked her mother, passing in the hall. Lady Darby popped her head in, her blonde hair pulled back in a modest twist. Her blue eyes alert.

Mattie's mind went blank. She couldn't tell her mother the truth. Instead, she stared at her like a deer in the line of fire.

"Lady Matilda has come up with a brilliant idea. She will write down some topics of conversation for next Season and practice her answers. Then, when her shyness tries to take over, the words will still come out." Franny smiled at Lady Darby. "We were hoping you could help us with the dialogue."

Mattie saw the tenderness in her mother's eyes, listening to Franny's altered version of the truth. It was times like this when Mattie knew her mother did truly love her. She had a hard shell, but beneath it, Mama had a deep affection for her children.

"A splendid idea." Lady Darby moved down the hall, still pondering the idea. "We will devise one for the weather, the last event to have taken place, and…"

"Thank you, Franny. She took me by surprise and my mouth refused to open." She gave her maid another quick hug. Something else the two of them hid from Lady Darby. The countess would never have approved of a close friendship between the two.

* * *

TWO DAYS *later at the musicale*

. . .

MATTIE SAT in the hot room, listening to Miss Rapperton torture the ivories of the pianoforte. There were at least three dozen fans flapping back and forth at high speed. The audience wore the same tolerant smile pasted on their faces. She prayed the next presentation would be better.

"I'm tempted to put my fingers in my ears," whispered Nicholas, on her left. "I can't believe you talked me into this."

"Papa once told me how he would bring scraps of cloth and stuff them in his ears when Mama would drag him to the opera," she whispered back.

"You could have shared that bit of information before we left," he replied with a dig of his elbow.

Mattie traced the embroidered pattern on the edges of her cream-colored shawl. It hadn't been a needed accessory, but it gave her hands something to fiddle with. She had worn her mother's choice of a simple Pomona muslin with a sash of darker green about the high waist. Thankfully, her hair was twisted into a chignon, leaving her nape bare to any stray breeze which might make an appearance through the floor-to-ceiling windows.

Applause erupted when the hostess's daughter finished.

"We mustn't clap too loudly, or she'll try to play another," her mother hissed in Mattie's ear. "I'm realizing how fortunate I am to have a daughter who is at least capable in everything she attempts."

Mattie warmed at the compliment. Considering Mama's temperament, it was high praise indeed. Since her mother had heard about "the plan," there had been a change in her demeanor. The defensive tone was gone. And she was enjoying this milder version of Lady Darby. Over the last two days, they had actually enjoyed each other's company.

When the last performer had finished, Darby leaned over. "We must get out of here. Would you join me for a walk in the garden?"

"Thank you," she agreed in a rush. "Mama, I'm going with Nicholas for a stroll in the garden."

"Don't be gone long. I cannot stay in this heat for too much longer." Lady Darby gave Mattie's arm a squeeze and moved toward a group of guests surrounding the hostess.

Her brother took her around a lovely, shaded walk. "Oh, this feels heavenly compared to the crowded music room. I'm still a little shocked you agreed to come, Nicky. Is it guilt?"

He nodded. "I have been gone a great deal. Hopefully, once the two smaller properties in the south are making a profit—or at least not costing us anything—I'll be able to spend more time at home. I've missed you, Sister."

She laid her head on his shoulder and hugged his arm as they ambled down the path. "Me, too."

"I have a question, hypothetical, to ask." She gave him a side-glance and saw his attention on her. "It goes without saying that I'm extremely tongue-tied when around other gentlemen."

"An understatement *and* a dilemma I've never understood. How many times have I wished for you to stop talking?" He looked to the sky as if asking a higher being. She slapped his arm.

"I'm serious. I need your opinion."

He stopped their progress and turned to face her. "I am all ears."

She laughed. "That puts the silliest image in my head."

Darby rolled his eyes. "Your question?"

"Suppose I met a gentleman, not of the *ton*, who I became friends with. Would it be terrible to run into him and enjoy his company on occasion?"

"Hypothetically, how would you meet this commoner?" His deep-blue eyes narrowed. "Where exactly would you like to meet him and why?"

49

Mattie spotted a bench and pulled her brother to it. She twisted her hands in her lap, then took a deep breath, and plunged in. "I met a man at St. James's Park. He saved a little boy from a swan attack, and then the swans went after him, so I intervened with my parasol to allow him to escape the lake, and then of course we had to invite him to share our blanket while he dried off." She stopped to drag in another breath, turning red when she noticed Nicholas's amused expression.

"So, you are wondering if you see him again at St. James's, would it be appropriate to speak with him again?"

She nodded. "Because of the odd situation, we've already met, though not officially."

"And your maid and Mr. Jones always accompany you?" he asked. "Do they know this gentleman?"

"Not before that day." Mattie wanted to keep Mr. Walters her secret, worrying if her mother found out, the friendship would end.

"Do you like him?"

"The truth is, Nicky, he is the first male not related to me who I could talk to without effort. He is not suitable for courting, but I thought if I practiced with him... Well, it would be easier when Mama is pushing me at men next spring." She blew out a loud breath. "It is not the same practicing with another woman."

"Perhaps if I met the man—"

"No, I don't want to scare him away. He's not in our social circle, though he's an upstanding man. I'm sure he would be intimidated by you." She grabbed his forearm with both her hands. "I thought to keep this my secret, but I cannot hide anything from you, Nicky."

"Do you promise never to be alone with him?" he asked, covering her hands with his and studying her intently. "The maid and driver will always be next to you?"

"Of course." Hope swelled in her chest. "I am glad I told you."

"Keep any conversations to under a half hour or less. *If* you cross paths again."

She leaned up to kiss him on the cheek. "Thank you, Nicky. I will."

* * *

THAT NIGHT she went to bed with images of Mr. Walters haunting her when she closed her eyes. She dreamt he was a medieval soldier who saved her from the enemy. Her uncle, the king, knighted Mr. Walters and told him to ask any favor in return for saving Lady Matilda.

If I can truly have anything, I would take your niece as my wife.

Mattie threw her arms around the newly appointed knight and kissed him. The touch of his mouth sizzled her lips, and she drew in her breath. His kiss was tender yet demanding. Bold yet subtle. The love in his eyes brought tears to hers. He twirled her round and round, proclaiming to the court he would have the most beautiful bride in all the land.

Mattie woke with the sheets twisted about her. She wiped the tears from her cheeks and smiled, gazing out at the moon glinting through the open window.

At least she could have Mr. Walters in her dreams.

Then another thought occurred to her.

How could she ever look him in the eye again after such a kiss?

CHAPTER 7

Three days later
The Grapes Tavern
Narrow Street, Limehouse

$\mathcal{W}$alters pushed through the crowd of dockworkers, sailors, and local patrons. The Grapes was a working-class tavern, and he fit in well, dressed as a sailor with his canvas slops and short dark jacket. He'd added a large mustache tonight. His wool cap was pulled well over his head, hiding most of his hair.

He liked using this tavern to meet up, depending on the client. First, it was far enough away from his own neighborhood, and second, much of the clientele came and went with the tide. Many here only patronized the Limehouse area when their ship was docked on the Thames. The Grapes' ideal location on the riverfront, next to the Limehouse docks and basin, made it popular with any crew. There were warehouses behind this street for storing the latest shipments and the merchandise waiting to go out. The scent of unwashed bodies and ale invaded his nose as he made his way toward the kegs.

Spotting George Edwards in a far corner, he pushed his way to the counter and waited for the barkeep to draw two bumpers. He counted out the amount of coins carefully, as if was making sure not to overpay the man. Generous men, or those with a heavy pocket, would draw attention here and become a mark when they left.

"Walters," the spy acknowledged as Harry sat down on the bench. "I heard you're to keep me alive."

Walters handed him one of the ales. "How many have you had?"

"Two," Edwards answered, reaching for the bumper. "I wanted to hold the table but be careful. This barley broth already has me mellow."

"Is there anything you need me to do? Besides watching out for your hide?" Walters took only a sip, knowing it would also be sour. He was getting spoiled in his old age with the fine ale served at the Dog's Bone and Paddy's excellent whiskey.

Edwards shook his head. "I still can't get Thistlewood to say who is funding the group. He calls him a concerned benefactor but won't give out his name."

"Keep trying. That information is priority."

"He trusts me, but there are many in the group who don't." Edwards leaned forward. "I know Colvin is a go-between, but if Thistlewood won't speak his name, we have no proof."

"Another shipment of weapons was purchased, mostly pistols and grenades. I'm trying to find out where they are stored. Thistlewood keeps information close to the chest, doesn't even tell the oldest members." Edwards pulled his worn cap lower, hiding his dark eyes. "I think when I get him alone, I may be able to learn the address. Over a year, and he's finally beginning to trust me."

Walters nodded. "Then we can surveil the building. If you need anything or need to meet with me, send word to the Dog's Bone. Leo is a friend of mine and will make sure I get the message."

Edwards grinned. "*Anything* is a broad term."

"Pertaining to the Spenceans only, please. When do you meet with the Philanthropists again?" Walters was ready to exit the crowded tavern.

"Next Tuesday, nine o'clock. You know where? On Cato Street?" he asked.

Walters nodded. "I'll be there. Remember, if you ever need to escape during a meeting, if things go awry, I will be the hackney driver waiting in the back. There's a public house close by, so if anyone tries to engage me, I'll say I'm taking care of a customer who's at The Horse and Groom."

Edwards nodded and rose to leave. "By the way, nice lip hair. Didn't recognize you until you sat down."

"Good. That's the point."

Walters waited until Edwards was gone, then headed toward the door, weaving his way through the patrons inside and surrounding the entrance outside. They were a raucous bunch tonight. He patted his sides, felt the reassuring solid butt of his pistols tucked inside his belt on each side. In addition, there was a knife in his boot and another up his left sleeve. Besides the drunken sailors here, these were neighborhoods only a prepared man would walk through at night.

He made his way up Narrow Street, planning to turn onto Lennox, then toward Commercial Street. There would be plenty of hackneys on the main road. He would arrive at the Theatre Royal just as Colvin was leaving.

Walters heard a scuffle and voices as he approached the next alley. Three men surrounded another, circling their victim.

"Give i' up, lad," rasped one. "No one fights so hard fer sixpence. Ye 'ave to have more to take such a beatin'."

As Walters eased into the dark alley, the ground glinting wet from the sudden light of the moon, the men closed in on their victim. The boy, his face bloody and swollen, left arm hanging at his side, swung his right arm. Bone crunched as the boy's fist connected with one of the thieves, and the man crumpled to the ground.

"Well, tha' weren't very polite, son. I think ye need to learn some manners," sneered one of the remaining men.

"I agree about the manners," said Walters, moving into the darkness, his pistol drawn. "Now, let's even up the numbers, shall we?" He clicked the hammer on his weapon.

"Bloody h—" Another crack of bone, and the waif sent another man falling to the slimy alley floor with a *thunk*.

The last man standing looked at the boy, then to Walters, and put out his hands. He inched sideways until he was facing Walters across the alley, then tried to run. Walters reached out and grabbed the man by his shirt collar, ducking right to avoid the flying fist as the thief struggled to get away.

A blow to his gut knocked the wind from him, but he still had enough strength to bring the butt of his pistol down on his attacker's head. Walters took a moment, his hands on his knees, pistol still at the ready, and caught his breath. He looked sideways at the boy, standing like a sapling in the wind, swaying side to side.

"What's your name, boyo?" he asked, approaching him slowly. There were two bodies behind the lad, just beginning to stir. The devil if the boy hadn't taken two down before Walters had arrived.

"Roger Lynch." He fell forward, and Walters caught him.

The boy was in bad shape, and Walters didn't think he could survive another beating. He looped the boy's right arm over his neck and walked him back to Narrow Street.

"If you can hear me, Roger, we're going to pretend you're drunk, and I'm bringing you home." Looking both ways and seeing nothing to warrant concern, Walters resumed his original direction. But now he was heading home—and to the O'Briens—instead of Covent Garden. He hoped the duke didn't have too "exciting" of an evening since Walters wouldn't be there to report it.

Walters had made it to the next corner when his new friend went completely slack. With a heavy sigh, he hoisted the boy onto his shoulder. He didn't weigh much, considering how he basted those tag-rags with that facer. A bloody mess over sixpence. Maggie would be in a temper when Walters brought this bundle home.

Once he reached Commercial Street, he set Roger against a wall and hailed a hackney. "Give me half a minute while I fetch something," he told the driver. He pulled Roger up and over his shoulder, put him in the coach, and yelled the address to the driver.

"Gracechurch, it is," the driver yelled back in acknowledgment.

When the hackney crossed into Cheapside and stopped in front of his house, Walters paid the man and retrieved Roger. He entered the hall with the boy over his shoulder.

"Maggie, Paddy, I need help." He paused, then added, "And send for Sampson."

Commotion from above confirmed the couple heard him, and he headed to the kitchen, which often served as a makeshift surgery. Sampson kept supplies there for times such as these.

Walters grabbed a covered bowl with rising dough and

set it on a chair before lowering Roger onto the table. He took off the boy's ragged coat to inspect for any gaping wounds. His left arm had been slashed and would need sewing, but no other major injuries on his upper body he could see. That would be for Dr. Brooks to determine.

"What has ye home so early and hollering—" Maggie stopped at the doorway, seeing the boy on the table, then sped into action. She went to the hearth and stoked the fire, grabbed some cloth, and joined Walters. "Let me take a look."

"Is there anyone to send for Sam?"

"I'm on my way. Where'd ye find him?" asked Paddy, pulling on a coat. "Took a pummeling, eh?"

"I was leaving The Grapes after meeting with Edwards. Three ruffians had him surrounded." Walters shook his head. "The lad held his own for a while. There were two down before I came upon the scene. He's got guts."

"Well, let's hope his guts ain't too badly damaged. Do yer best, love." Paddy put on his cap and stopped at the back door. "Tar anseo!" he called to his dog.

"I feel better when he takes the filthy beast with him," Maggie mumbled, her attention on the lad. "Few men brave enough to challenge a gargantuan pair such as dem."

Maggie peeled off the boy's shirt and applied a cold, wet cloth to the oozing wound. She *tsked* as she went to work, occasionally smoothing back the boy's rat's nest of black curls and murmuring soothing words to him.

"I doubt if he can hear you," Walters said as he moved his hands up and down Roger's legs, checking for any breaks. He removed the shoes—if one could call them that—untying the thick string holding the two large remnants of worn leather together. A small pouch fell to the floor.

"What is it, Harry?"

He shook it and heard the coins jingle. There *had* been

more to steal. "The money he didn't want the thieves to find. He fought hard enough for it."

"I hope he lives to enjoy it." She turned back to her patient. "Let's get him cleaned up for Sam."

By the time Sampson and Paddy returned, the boy was stripped down to his drawers with a sheet pulled over him. His arm was lightly bandaged, ready for the physician.

"What have you found so far?" Sampson asked, removing his hat to reveal neatly combed brown hair, stylishly cut. His hazel eyes quickly took stock of his patient.

"Only this gash on his arm," answered Maggie. "But he's been out for some time, according to Harry, so I'm worried about a whack to da noggin or something hurt on da inside."

"Any blood from his mouth, nose, or ears?" Dr. Brooks's capable hands moved up and down the body, stopping here or there for a better inspection.

Walters and Maggie both shook their heads.

"That's good." Sam unwrapped the arm bandage and whistled. "Quite a cut. Do you have the water ready?"

Maggie nodded and went to the kettle over the fire. Paddy pulled out a bottle of Irish whiskey and handed it to Sam, who poured it over the wound.

"For all that's holy!" Roger's lids blinked open, hissing in pain. He pinned his green eyes on Walters, rasping, "Am I dead?"

Walters laughed. "I hope not, or you took me with you."

The yelling roused Paddy's dog, and he sat beside the patient, two giant paws on the table. The lad let out a gasp.

"Síos leat!" scolded Maggie, glaring at the hound as put his paws back on the floor. "Amach leat!" And the dog left the kitchen to lie in the hall and wait for his master, his brown soulful eyes watching their every move.

．　．　．

"QUIET, BOYO," said Paddy, lifting Roger's upper body and offering him the whiskey. "Ye'll be wanting a wee drink o' dis before da good doctor gets to work."

If the boy had been pale before, he went full white now. After a nod, Paddy lowered it to his lips, and Roger took several big gulps.

"Seems ye're no stranger to da bottle," murmured Paddy with amusement. "One more for good measure."

Sampson finished preparing the injury for stitches, threaded the needle, and nodded to Paddy, who took the boy's hand in his. "Ye squeeze my hand as hard as ye need. Yell like a banshee if ye want. No one here will care."

Walters was impressed. Roger never whimpered, just clamped his jaw tight and held on to Paddy's huge paw. Maggie wiped the boy's forehead with a cool cloth.

"Fifteen. And a fine job if I do say so myself." Sampson stepped back and surveyed his handiwork. "Must have been protecting something important to risk your life."

Roger leaned up. "Where'r me boots?" Panic shone in his gray-green eyes.

"Is that what you call them?" Harry held up the leather pieces.

"Tell me ye have me pouch of coins."

Harry held it up. "This?"

Roger fell back against the table, a smile on his face before he passed out again.

Paddy took a drink from the bottle. "He's a wee older than what we usually take in. What d'ye t'ink, Maggie, my love?"

"I t'ink we should see if he has a mother of his own, ye old curmudgeon. I'm getting too old for raising boys." She put her arm around her husband's waist and looked at Sampson and Walters. "I'm saving my energy for our grandchildren."

"That is my cue to leave," declared Sampson, his dimple

deepening as he grinned at Harry and collected his equipment. "As the eldest, I believe you should show your younger siblings the way to matrimonial bliss."

"Come, Harry. We'll drink away yer worries in the library."

CHAPTER 8

October, the following week
Royal Academy of Art

"*L*ady Matilda, stop tapping your foot. You'll work up a sweat and smell like a scullery maid before he arrives." Franny put a hand on one hip.

"I don't see anything wrong with the smell of scullery maids," said Mr. Jones from above them. "I'm courtin' one."

Franny said, rolling her eyes, "It was just an example of a hardworking person."

Mr. Jones grunted in reply, then turned on the driver's bench to face their pair of matched grays and the majestic steeple of St. Mary le Strand. Mattie began pacing beside the curricle instead. She wore a violet muslin dress with an ivory sash and lace trim. Her straw bonnet was adorned with small ivory and purple flowers and tied beneath her chin with a violet ribbon. Loose pale-blonde curls fell over her cheeks, bouncing as she took each anxious step.

In front of them was the grand Royal Academy of Art, a Palladian-style, six-story building of light stonework. Nine arches on the first level supported Corinthian columns along the second. Shielding her eyes from the sun, Mattie studied the figures of Justice, Truth, Valour, and Moderation, standing across the attic level. They each held their related symbols of scales, mirror, sword, and bridle, standing watch over the facade beneath the many windows glinting in the afternoon light. Situated on the summit was John Bacon the Elder's sculpture of the figures from *Fame* and the *Genius of England* supporting the British arms.

"It's a magnificent place, isn't it?" remarked Franny. "And the wonders inside are open to all of us."

"It would take weeks to pay all the exhibits the attention they are due," agreed Mattie.

"So where would you like to begin?" asked a deep tenor behind her.

"Oh!" squeaked Mattie, a hand flying to her pounding heart. "How do you manage to sneak up on me like that?"

"You were paying attention to something else." He wore a forest-green day coat, a waistcoat of a slightly lighter shade, and fawn-colored trousers. He took off his beaver hat and swept her a bow. "Forgive me for the fright."

I could forgive such a handsome man anything, she thought. Instead, she gushed, "I'm just happy you were able to make it."

He offered her his arm, and they walked through the arches of the Royal Academy of Art with Franny following behind. Mr. Walters paid the modest entrance fee for their group despite Mattie's protest. Turning east, Mattie marveled again at the Navy Stair that wound its way to the top of the building and led to the Naval Board Rooms.

"Have you decided what subject you would like to attempt today, Lady Matilda?"

She pressed her lips together, pushing back the urge to say, "You." Franny was right in saying Mattie could easily scare him away. The way he had spoken her name was an instant reminder of their class difference. She pushed the thought to the back of her mind and began the topic of the weather. When they arrived at the first gallery, she heard Franny gasp behind her.

Mattie couldn't blame her maid. It was a bit overwhelming. Paintings were hung right next to each other in rows, from eye level almost to the ceiling. Those above their heads were tilted at an angle for better viewing. There were half-moon-shaped windows above, allowing natural light to brighten the room.

The conversation turned to art, and she found Mr. Walters had an appreciation for the classics.

"I enjoy portraitures," Mattie said. "The idea of someone's image lasting throughout time."

"So no one will forget you?"

"Exactly!" She grinned at him, a thought occurring to her. "What would you like to be remembered for?"

His eyes widened in surprise at the question. "Hmm, I'm not sure if I care whether I'm remembered in a hundred years. But for those who know me, I would hope they remember I was a fair man, one who did his best to make this world a better place."

"What do you do for a living, Mr. Walters? Something which will help you achieve this goal?" They were friends now, so it seemed appropriate to ask a more personal question.

"I work for my father's agency. He... finds things that people need or have lost." He smiled at her, making her stomach tumble. "It can be very rewarding."

"What kind of things?" Did his father own a merchant

ship? Did he carry goods, locate expensive items or anti-quaries?

"It depends." He pointed to a landscape. "Do you enjoy landscapes?"

She tilted her head, considering the one in front of her depicting the English countryside. "If they have a living being within, people or animals rather than just hills, fields, and trees. I like seeing the livestock that would be grazing and not just the pasture. The people who are having a picnic rather than just the park."

"You appreciate life. It suits you."

She laughed. "A compliment, good sir?"

"Indeed. Those who do are usually compassionate toward their fellow man and understanding of other cultures." His brown eyes held hers. "I believe society is often cruel when confronting anything different from what they know or believe. It's a shame. So many immigrants are treated poorly because their native language shapes their speech."

Their conversation was taking a more serious turn. "Yes, I agree with that assumption. Rejecting or ridiculing someone or something because you don't understand it, creates a shallow person who closes off so many opportunities for learning."

"And you enjoy learning."

"It's the thorn in my mother's side. I would rather enjoy a good book than spend an afternoon making inane conversation with a man who couldn't care less about me." She gasped. "I apologize. It was a rude comment."

"Speaking the truth is not rude, Lady Matilda. I admire a forthright person."

Her cheeks warmed, but before she could respond, he turned to Franny. "And what type of art do you prefer, Miss Tilbot?"

"Oh, I love the sculptures, sir. Thank you for asking," Franny said, beaming at the inclusion.

Mattie realized Mr. Walters was closer to her maid in class. He could just as easily be here as Franny's companion. The thought sent a flash of jealousy through her. *Stop it*, she scolded herself. *No romantic notions, for it will only lead to trouble.* "Shall we move on to the sculptures?"

The afternoon passed quickly. She found Mr. Walters to be discriminating in his tastes, and much more knowledgeable than she'd assumed. He also made sure to bring Franny into their conversations. "Were you formally educated, Mr. Walters?"

He chuckled. "Educated, yes. Formally, no. My mother taught me to read and write before I attended public school. I learned to use the library to satisfy my curiosity on other subjects that interested me."

"Your interests must be quite varied, then," she said, admiring his profile as they headed toward the exit.

"Lady Matilda, there's a cart selling refreshment. Are you thirsty?" asked Franny when they emerged from the Academy.

"Allow me, ladies," intervened Mr. Walters. "What would you like?"

"Lemonade, please," Mattie said, realizing how dry her mouth was from all this conversation. Franny echoed her agreement.

He returned, holding three cups between his large hands. The ladies each took one, and he held his cup up. "To an excellent day with lovely company."

Both women blushed, though Mr. Walters's umber eyes stayed on her. She had the oddest feeling he knew more about her than she realized. Ridiculous, of course, for they had only spent hours together. Then again, she had been comfortable with him from the moment they met.

The lemonade was quite good and a perfect ending to the afternoon. Mr. Walters escorted them back to the curricle, where Mr. Jones was speaking with two women. His hat was tucked under his arm, his dark curls mussed, and his free hand moved about as he spoke. Both ladies appeared quite taken with the handsome driver.

When Mr. Jones saw them, he bowed to the women, who giggled and went on their way. He pulled down the steps of the conveyance and opened the door, his eyes growing wide when Mr. Walters held out his hand from the opposite side.

"May I?" he asked Franny and helped her into the curricle.

"Lady Matilda," Mr. Walters turned to her, holding out his hand.

She placed her gloved hand in his, wishing he was joining them in the carriage. "Can we take you home?"

"I'm afraid I have business to attend. Besides, it wouldn't be proper."

"Will you meet with me again?"

Mattie saw the hesitation but gave him her most brilliant smile when he agreed. "Wonderful. Could we visit the Royal Menagerie?"

Franny let slip an excited "oh" and Mattie laughed.

"I've only gone once," Mr. Walters agreed, "so it would be a pleasure."

"Same time next week?"

He nodded, tipped his hat, then walked away. Mattie watched his figure disappear down the street, wondering if he had a romantic interest. Not that it was any of her concern, of course.

* * *

THE BUTLER OPENED the door for them as soon as the curricle stopped in front of the Darby townhouse. She hurried up the portico steps and smiled at Mr. Hamley, who nodded in return. "Lady Darby would like to see you in her sitting room."

"Oh." Mattie hoped her mother wasn't upset with her. Had she found out where she'd gone? "Thank you, I'll go right up." She handed her bonnet to Franny and took the stairs to the second floor.

"Hello, Mama," she said, bending to give her mother a kiss on the cheek. "Did you want to see me?"

The smile Mattie received eased her mind. Again, she marveled at how well they were getting along lately. Perhaps she wanted to have another practice at conversation.

"A friend of mine is visiting London. I haven't seen her in years, though we've corresponded regularly. She's here with her son, and I've invited them for dinner at the end of the week." Her mother leaned forward and patted Mattie's arm. "This will be an excellent chance for you."

A knot formed in her belly. "Of course, Mama."

"I will ask your brother to attend, but other than that, I'll keep it small." Her mother's blue eyes held kindness.

"Thank you, Mama, for your understanding. And I will do my best to be entertaining and charming." She would. After an afternoon with Mr. Walters, she truly felt as if she could.

"I know you will, my dear." Lady Darby cleared her throat, a nervous expression on her still pretty face. "Would you like to... go to Hatchards tomorrow with me? The fashion magazines are coming out with the upcoming winter styles. I thought I'd purchase the latest *La Belle Assemblée*."

"Oh, Mama, I'd love to." Mattie's heart swelled. They were meeting in the middle. She would talk with young men, and her mother would go with her to the bookstore. "Shall we have tea?"

With a broad smile, she yanked the bellpull and said a silent prayer for mute swans.

CHAPTER 9

Late October
Gracechurch Street

"I'd like to thank ye again for the opportunity," Roger said, crumpling his cap in his hands, his gray-green eyes studying the pattern of the wool rug beneath his feet. The lanky young man seemed ill at ease in the O'Brien parlor. "First, ye save me hide, then ye give me proper work. It's like bein' waylaid was a miracle for Ma and me."

Walters hid his grin. It turned out Roger Lynch was almost sixteen. The pouch he'd hidden in his boot was the rent money for the room he shared with his mother and two younger siblings. No wonder he'd have fought to the death. His family would have been evicted.

"You heal fast," remarked Walters. The boy's face was still bruised, but the swelling had receded, and scabs had formed over any scrapes. He moved his left arm gingerly but insisted it was fine.

"He's young." Paddy tousled the lad's black hair and walked to the side table to pour a finger of whiskey. "Ain't no favor, boyo. Ye work for it or get my foot up yer backside."

"Yessir. When can I start?"

"Would you like to know your wage?" asked Harry. He'd asked around about the boy and found he was a hard worker and honest. The father had been run over by a hackney five years ago, and he'd been helping to take care of the family ever since. When he'd seen the boarding house Roger lived in, heard of the landlord's reputation, Walters knew how easy it would be to make this family's life better.

Roger blinked, then shrugged. "Any income Ma and me can depend on is good."

"I'll start ye at a shilling a day. You'll be our gip, do whatever we need—running errands, hauling barrels, shopping with Mrs. O'Brien." Paddy threw back the whiskey and smiled, peering down at Roger. "I may need ye five days a week or seven, depending on the week. Is dat acceptable?"

"Anything ye need, Mr. O'Brien, Mr. Walters. I'm yer man." Roger's eyes held hope. Hope for a decent wage, decent lodgings for his family, clothes, and food on the table. "Me ma does the best she can, washing clothes, mending, but ain't never enough. And with winter comin' on…"

"Well, ye work hard, boyo, and ye'll get a wee raise when ye turn sixteen." Paddy gave Harry a wink as he reached down to scratch his dog's ears. "Let's see what he's made of, aye?"

"Aye," agreed Walters. "Now go tell your mother to look for better lodgings." He watched Roger back out of the parlor, murmuring more thanks. What was wrong with this world that the evil are able to thrive while the good must scrape to survive?

"He'll be as handy as a skillet in da kitchen," boomed Paddy, breaking into his thoughts. "We did a good t'ing, Harry. Saved more than just a lad today, saved an entire family."

"Aye, but I wish we could do more."

"We are. By going after men like da Duke of Colvin, we eliminate them who take advantage of da destitute." Paddy clasped Harry's shoulder. "'Tis a never-ending battle, ye know. We ain't got da luxury o' giving up."

Walters shook his head. "No, we don't. You taught me that a long time ago. Sometimes, though, it would be nice to see we're making a mark."

"You go to da Lynch's new place when dey find it. Ye'll see da mark we're making."

* * *

Early November
  St. Giles, near Seven Dials

THE FOG WAS HEAVY TONIGHT, soaking into his coat, covering any skin showing. The light breeze only served to move the mist around, so at times, Walters could see the door of the building, and then it was blurred. Paddy's words echoed in his brain as he shivered. The cobblestones were slick, making it difficult to run if needed.

We ain't got da luxury o' giving up.

No, they didn't. Colvin had moved his carnal desires out of Covent Garden and across Long Acre—closer to Seven Dials. The house the duke presently visited was known for catering to customers with special requests. An adventuress here charged extra for "exotic tastes."

The man was courting the devil. Walters looked up at the

weak light showing from some of the windows. This entire street was given up to "nunneries," gaming hells, and gin houses. He pulled the collar of his wool coat more snugly around his neck and stomped his feet against the chill of the evening. He might blend in better wearing a working man's dress, but he certainly wasn't warmer.

A hackney turned onto the street, the horses' hooves echoing against the stone, their breath sending puffy clouds to merge with the fog. It stopped in front of the house, and Colvin emerged. Walters moved quietly behind the conveyance, listening for the direction. He heard the duke give the address of his townhouse. His tone was jovial, so he must have gotten what he wanted. Nausea rolled through Walters, not wanting to think what the man considered enjoyable.

He'd report to Darby when the earl returned to Town. Tomorrow he would take his turn surveilling the earl's house. And his sister. This little scheme of hers had blown into something much larger than he'd imagined. They had been meeting weekly at small museums or small parks off the main thoroughfares, but never any place where she would be easily recognized.

On their first visit to the Royal Menagerie, Lady Matilda had been stopped by a friend of her mother's. Walters had wandered off and learned later that Miss Tilbot had claimed him as her beau. He didn't like the deception but realized the necessity.

Another unhappy consequence was his growing attraction to Lady Matilda. It could lead nowhere except heartache for both of them. He recognized the desire, and often hope, in her clear blue eyes. They reflected his own. But he was glad he could help her.

Their meetings had indeed given her confidence with the

opposite sex. She claimed to have entertained dinner guests at her home several times now. Lady Darby was pleased with her daughter's progress, and Walters knew he must cut it off soon. The disappointment he would see on her face hurt his heart, but his hands were tied.

Just as he reached the corner, casting his gaze about the dark streets for a hackney to hail, he heard more voices coming out of the brothel. He looked over his shoulder and thought he recognized them. The man with the dark hair had been one of those involved in the insurance fraud. The scheme that had brought down his brother, Sampson's, father. The other had attended the last few Spencean meetings on Cato Street.

Walters turned the corner and ducked inside an alcove smelling of urine. The men passed by him, continuing across the street. He waited a few moments, then followed them.

"They've got another shipment comin' in next week to Mother Abby's in Seven Dials. We'll let the delivery get settled, then see 'ow many we can pilfer. The Vicar wants us to sell 'em to Molly's in Whitechapel. If Abby gets 'er usual half dozen, she'll split 'em up. We can sneak in through the alley and nab the ones kept off the kitchen." The dark-haired man peered at his friend. "Ye ain't thinkin' of backin' out, are ye?"

The other man shook his head. "No, Robert. I just don't want to get caught. I got a family to support."

"Like I don't?"

Robert Dunn, that was his name. What was he up to? The evening was taking an interesting turn. Was the man working for Colvin? Could this be the link to connect the duke with the Spenceans?

"Sure, ye've got a wife," said the other man. "But I got four tykes. They'll starve if I get caught."

"Ye're workin' for the Vicar, now. He pays high wages. That comes with risks. Ye knew this when I brought ye in. Don't start whinin' just because things get a little thick." Dunn elbowed his friend before turning in another direction. "I'll see ye next week. Give the missus my regards."

Walters stopped following the men, going over what he'd heard. What were they up to? Stealing a shipment of goods and reselling them. But what would a brothel be ordering?

Liquor, of course.

But who was the vicar they worked for? He shook his head. A man of God making a profit from stolen alcohol. Unbelievable. He'd pass this on to his brother, Gus. Between Colvin and the Spenceans, Walters had little time left in a day. Gus had just finished a case and could take over Robert Dunn's trail. He'd also give Sampson another update when they met for their weekly breakfast.

* * *

THE NEXT NIGHT, Walters walked along the crescent of townhouses. Made of pale-yellow limestone, they seemed like a beacon in the night, standing tall and wanting to be seen. He wore his old coat, his shoulders hunched, and cap pulled low over his eyes. He passed by Darby's portico with its deep-red door flanked by pillars and a carved plaster pineapple above the entrance. It was a beautiful home with bow windows gracing each side of the structure.

He made his way around to the back lane, stopping at the mews behind the small garden of Darby's townhouse. The earl was away, and though he'd begun training Roger for surveillance, Walters didn't want the boy on his own for a while yet. It was an unusually warm night for early November. The moon was full, and a slight breeze rustled the leaves of the tree above him. A narrow alley laid the boundary for the end of the properties along this street, and several homes had built mews to house their carriages and horses.

"I will, Mama. It's just so beautiful out tonight that I thought I'd sketch the garden in the moonlight."

His heart pounded in his ears. Lady Matilda found a spot on a stone bench and opened the familiar drawing pad on her lap. She wore a dark gown with long sleeves but no bonnet or cap. A heavy shawl warmed her shoulders. Moonbeams danced across her pale hair. *Spun gold*, he thought. She was so beautiful, inside and out.

She volunteered at the hospital and treated Miss Tilbot and Mr. Jones more like friends rather than servants. Class divide did not affect her view of people. When she looked at him, he felt ten feet tall, as if he could do anything.

Down the narrow cobblestone path, he saw a group of men in front of the mews at the end of the lane. Probably footmen or stable boys, loud enough to indicate the young men weren't sneaking about. He stepped behind a tree instead of his usual spot in the shadow of the small stable, dressed in his usual disguise for this duty in Hanover Square. Even if the group spotted him, he doubted they would make much of a harmless old man. He turned his attention back to Lady Matilda and admired the arch of her back, the curve of her slender neck. If they lived in a different world—

Lady Matilda stopped sketching and sat up straight, her head moving back and forth. She shivered, a delicate movement that made him want to wrap his arms around her. He imagined coming up behind her, placing his lips on her ivory neck, kissing along her jaw, slowly making his way to her mouth. The only time he'd touched her—more than a hand on hers, tucked in his elbow as they walked—had been during their second visit to the Royal Menagerie.

. . .

"*THEY ARE SUCH BEAUTIFUL BEASTS*," *Lady Matilda said as they passed the lion.*

"Though I hate to see them caged and teased." Walters always hated seeing a wild animal contained, stolen from their natural habitat. "They are majestic beasts, kings of their homeland."

Two women and a small boy approached the cage. Walters and Lady Matilda watched as the women chatted and ignored the youngster. He had pulled half a meat pie from his pocket. He held it toward the lion, who moved closer and began to sniff the air. As the animal approached, the boy dropped a stick from his sleeve, carved to a tip at one end.

As the lion came near the bars, the boy struck out with his stick. The lion let out a low rumble, attracting the attention of the women.

"I told you not to tease the animals," scolded one woman, then returned to her conversation.

The boy grinned, saw the women were again distracted, and held out the meat pie again. When he lifted his hand with the stick, Lady Matilda stepped in front of the lad and snatched the boy's weapon.

At the same time, the lion's huge paw came through the bars above Lady Matilda's head. Walters surged forward and pulled her away, just as the beast's claws came down, ripping the shawl she wore.

She tumbled into his chest with a squeak, and his arms went around her by instinct. When she gazed at him, fear and... trust?... in her ocean-blue eyes, lips trembling, his heart surrendered. It took all his self-control not to press his mouth to hers.

"IS ANYONE THERE?" She stood now, walking toward the back of the garden.

Had she heard the men at the end of the lane? Or had she

sensed his presence? The latter thrilled and terrified him at the same time.

CHAPTER 10

"Only me," called Miss Tilbot, hurrying from the direction of the house. "Lady Darby wanted you to have your wool mantle. The shawl is much too thin for this weather."

The maid arranged a dark swath of material about her mistress's shoulders. From behind, Walters could hear the stable boys coming closer. It was after eight, so they must be going home for the night if their employers were staying at home.

"What are you sketching tonight, miss?" asked Miss Tilbot, taking a peek at the drawing pad.

"I'm trying to draw the ship we saw on the Thames the other day." Lady Matilda laughed. "But when I looked up at that moon, I got caught up in its magic and couldn't concentrate."

"I've always thought of it as romantic. It's so beautiful and seems so close, yet is far beyond our reach," mused Miss Tilbot.

"It's how I feel about love," Lady Matilda said in a breathy voice. She shivered again and squinted, peering into the clump of trees where Walters hid.

At the same time, the group of young men passed him, then stopped at the garden gate.

"If fortune ain't favoring us," slurred a short man with a bulbous nose. "Two bee-oo-tiful ladies waitin' fer us."

The maid pulled on Lady Matilda's cape, trying to get her away from the gawking men. The tall thin man reached out and snatched Lady Matilda's arm.

"Not so fast, ladies," he said. "My mates here just want to have a chat. Or aren't we good enough fer ye?"

The third and fourth men laughed but kept their distance, obviously not as drunk as the first two. Walters was torn. If he showed himself, he knew Lady Matilda would recognize him. He would have to explain why he was there and who he was working for. Her trust would be broken, and their friendship would end in betrayal and hatred. It would hurt more than living without her.

Bulbous Nose blew out a loud breath and reached out to touch Lady Matilda's hair. His breath must have been heavy with drink because she wrinkled her nose and leaned away.

"Do not touch my mistress," snarled Miss Tilbot. "Be on your way, gentlemen."

"Gentlemen, she called us," said Skinny Man. "And we ain't doin' no harm. I think you should both give us a kiss." He lunged forward and grabbed Miss Tilbot's arm, pulling her against the fence.

Bulbous Nose put his hands on Lady Matilda's shoulders to do the same. "C'mon," moaned one of the two men in the background. "Ye'll get us fired. Leave 'em be."

"Shut yer bloody mouth or I'll shut it fer ye," grumbled Bulbous Nose, not taking his eyes off Lady Matilda. "Now, how 'bout a li'l kiss?"

Walters burst from his hiding place and plowed into the two drunken men. Skinny Man landed on the bottom of the pile, his head striking the cobblestones, and didn't move. Bulbous Nose struggled beneath Walters as he raised a fist and slammed it into the man's face. Blood spurted from the man's nose; the ladies screamed.

"Get 'im, ye bloody nodcocks, or ye'll be next," Bulbous Nose bellowed in a pained voice. The other two men jumped into action and pulled Walters from the pile. As they held him, Bulbous Nose slowly rose, pitching back and forth as he lunged at Walters, driving his fist into Walters's stomach.

Walters doubled over, still held by Bulbous Nose's friends. When he'd caught his breath, he looked up and received another punch to the gut. He vaguely heard Lady Matilda calling for help, then his body hit the cobblestones with a thud. A foot caught him in the head, and everything went black.

* * *

WHEN THE MAN grabbed her arms, Mattie screamed as loud as she could. Franny was flailing her arms at her attacker and slapped his face. Out of nowhere came a dark figure, flying through the air and toppling both their assailants. A sickening *thud* echoed as the taller man hit the stone and went silent.

Their timely hero got in a punch to the other man on the ground but was soon waylaid by the two friends who had stayed out of the ruckus until now. Then the stocky little man with the large red nose punched their champion in the stomach.

"Help! Someone help!" she cried loudly, both hands around her mouth to amplify the sound. "Mr. Jones, where are you? Help!"

Franny added her voice when the poor man received a second punch. Mr. Jones came running from their small stable, where he had a room above. His shirt was hanging loose, his pants sagging, and one boot on. He held a large stick in one hand and a pistol in the other.

"Stand down," he growled at the men. "Somebody's getting some lead in his gut, and the rest will have busted heads when I'm done." He waved the long, heavy piece of wood above his head.

Silence hung heavy in the air as the three men standing turned to look at Mr. Jones. If the situation wasn't so serious, the ruffians might have laughed at him. But there was murder in Mr. Jones's eyes that sent a chill down Mattie's back.

His chest rose and fell as he aimed the pistol and pulled back the hammer. *Click.* "Choose your poison." Silence hung heavy in the air for a moment, then chaos.

Mattie couldn't breathe. Time stopped as their assailants blinked, looking at one another, then at the unconscious man on the ground, and finally back at Mr. Jones. In silent agreement, the men ran, leaving their friend behind.

Mattie rushed through the gate to help the would-be hero who had come to their rescue. "Mr. Jones, please make sure the other man is not dead," she said in her calm hospital voice, though her hands trembled.

She pushed on their champion and tried to roll him over, but he was too heavy. Mattie got him to his side. He was breathing, but she couldn't see him well enough to tend him without more light. His coat was worn and—

A mended rip along the collar. It was the old man she'd seen several times. What was he doing here, and why had he tried to defend them by himself? Guilt rolled over her.

"He's alive," called Mr. Jones. "I'll get some rope and truss him before I go for the constable."

"Put him in the stable," added Franny, her face pale. "Lock him in a closet or something."

"Yes, ma'am."

"Bound the scalawag's hands and feet first, then come and help us get this poor man into the kitchen. When you go for the constable, send for a physician too." Mattie picked up the man's woolen cap and smoothed back his hair. Under the trees, she couldn't see his face well but knew he'd been kicked in the head.

At the mention of a physician, the man stirred.

"Don't move, sir. We are fetching help and will get you into the house in a moment," she told him in a soothing voice.

He shook his head. "No doctor."

"He can speak. That's a good sign, isn't it?" asked Franny.

Mattie had no idea. "Can you sit up?" She put her arm under his back, her other hand on his arm, and pulled him forward. The moon peeked out from a cloud, and she could see his face clearly. While the scruffy gray beard distracted her at first, his gaze did not.

Mr. Walters blinked, his deep-brown eyes hazy with pain.

She gasped. "Wh-what are you doing here?" Was he watching her at night? Did he follow her during the day? Apprehension skittered down her back. Not fear, for she knew he would never hurt her. But a wariness filled her chest. Something was not right.

Mr. Jones came to assist them and helped Mr. Walters to a standing position. "Well, ain't this a surprise," he said, seeing who the injured man was.

"Well, throw me in the Thames and tell me it's the ocean," whispered Franny.

As they made their way across the garden, Mattie cast a curious glance at her driver. "I didn't realize you were also trained as a bodyguard."

"A requirement his lordship insisted on when I was

hired," Mr. Jones answered with a grin. "I'm also not a bad pugilist. Got a wicked left punch."

Once in the kitchen, Franny went to work, putting a kettle on the hearth to heat water and finding cloths to help clean up Mr. Walters. Once they were settled, Mr. Jones left to move the tall man into the stable and fetch the constable.

Mr. Walters opened his mouth to say something, his eyes filled with pain and... remorse? She went to close the door leading to the hall, wanting to keep other staff from interrupting, but he leaned over to touch her arm. His grimace told her he might have a few broken ribs.

"Not now, Mr. Walters. Get your strength back while we nurse you, then we'll talk," she said, turning her back on him. Mattie blinked back tears, irritated with herself. *There must be a reasonable explanation.* But if there wasn't, she'd be devastated.

After closing the door, she searched for the cook's rum. Finding it in one of the cupboards, she took a cloth from the pile Franny had gathered and inspected Mr. Walters's head. "It seems you're quite good at getting caught in the middle of things," she murmured as she parted his hair where blood had welled up.

The thick waves against her fingers made her pause. She closed her eyes, realizing it was as soft as she'd imagined. Because she had imagined running her fingers through his hair, touching his cheeks, kissing his lips. Heat rushed through her as the images of her dreams came bursting forth. Her hand trembled for a moment.

He's just another patient, like the children at the hospital.

Except this patient was handsome as sin, with a broad chest, strong arms, and muscled thighs.

Carefully, she poured a bit of rum on the gash. He hissed but didn't move. "It will require a few stitches," she said, trying to keep the emotion from her voice. "You must see a physician."

"My brother is a doctor," he mumbled. "He'll tend me well enough."

"Quite a family you have," she said, moving to inspect his face. A bump on his head, probably where he hit the cobblestones. She dabbed it with rum, satisfied it wouldn't bleed, and moved on to his chin. "A sister on the stage, a brother in the medical field. What other family secrets are you hiding? Oh yes, you've mentioned a brother who is a solicitor."

He winced when she wiped his scraped chin a bit forcefully. She was torn between gratitude for helping her and Franny, and anger at lying to her about who he was. An old man, indeed.

"Four brothers, younger, are detectives like me"—he shot her glance, then stared at her hand holding the cloth—"one doctor, one solicitor. We were all waifs on the street when Paddy found us. He and Maggie gave us a home and raised us as their own."

Her expression softened at the last admission. "Only one sister?"

He nodded. "And an Irish wolfhound. My father owns O'Brien Investigative Service. It's a... family business."

"A wolfhound? Aren't they as tall as people?"

"Only if they stand on their hind legs, and then taller than most men."

"Is the dog also part of the 'family business'?"

Walters snorted, then regretted it as a wave of pain bounced around in his skull. "No. He's good protection, though."

Mattie stepped back, eyes narrowed as he studied his middle. "I'm afraid it wouldn't be proper to try to wrap your ribs until Mr. Jones returns."

"They aren't broken. I've had enough to know." He gave

her a sheepish look. "But if they are, Sampson will take care of it. Thank you for all you've done."

"You are welcome. Now, it's time for an explanation." *Please, please, let this sound reasonable.*

"I'm on a case now for your brother," he said. His gruff voice sounded unfamiliar. A tone she'd never heard before. "He wants to find evidence against—"

"No, tell me he isn't after that horrendous man."

"A duke."

Mattie sighed and sat down next to Mr. Walters. This made sense. "He's determined to get retribution for his dead wife. I wish he could just leave it be. The poor woman is gone and out of her misery. Yet he clings to his."

Her father had lost a fortune to the deceased Duke of Colvin. Everyone at the table knew the man had cheated, but no one could prove it. When their father died, Nicholas was left to deal with the debt.

Their mother had convinced him to marry her dear friend's daughter. With her generous dowry, the Darby title could be respected again. Her brother agreed on the condition the woman was willing. The girl was a beauty, and it seemed there would be a happy ending for all.

On their wedding night, Nicholas's wife had confided she was pregnant. The marriage was a sham, she'd been seduced by another peer, and promptly ignored. She had insisted it was her mother's idea, that the man in question would ruin them if they uncovered the scandal.

Nicholas had left her in a rage. When he had returned calm and ready to talk, he'd found her dead, unable to deal with the shame, and setting him free. She'd left a note, apologizing for the deception and naming the man. The Duke of Colvin's son.

"I thought he'd finally let it go," she murmured, tears

filling her eyes. "None of it was his fault, yet he cannot have a life until justice is found."

Mr. Walters sighed. "I tried to tell you that we shouldn't pursue our friendship. I'm so very sorry."

"Then why did you?" she blurted out.

"Because I cannot find a way to deny you anything." He reached out and put his hand over hers. "When your brother is away on business, I keep an eye on the townhouse if you are staying in London. It gives him peace of mind, knowing you are safe."

Mattie studied his hand atop hers. It seemed so natural for him to give her comfort. How could something that felt so right be wrong? When he lifted his hand, she was cold down to her soul. Not trusting her voice yet, she simply nodded.

"We both knew this was a temporary relationship. Neither of us fit into the other's world." He tipped her chin up, and she wanted to lean her cheek into his palm. "But know this, I wouldn't give up a moment of what we've shared."

Franny cleared her throat from outside the door leading to the garden. "Mr. Jones has returned with the constable."

"Let me talk to him and see if we can excuse you from making a statement. You've been through enough for one day," Mr. Walters said, rising with a groan. "Then we'll finish this conversation."

CHAPTER 11

*W*alters heaved a sigh of relief when the constable was a familiar face. He gave a description of the incident, explained that Lady Matilda was distraught, and promised to bring her statement to Bow Street the next day. Jones and Miss Talbot told the constable their versions, and the man was dragged away with assurances of keeping the crime quiet.

Walters would find out the names of the other men tomorrow. Skinny Man would surely give up the others or spend time in Newgate. His guess was the former. When he returned to the garden, he found Lady Matilda on the stone bench, her mantle wrapped around her again.

"Franny, you may wait for me in my bedchamber," she told her lady's maid in a no-argument tone. "Mr. Jones, thank you for your courage tonight. I will be sure my brother hears of it."

"Thank you, miss," he murmured before turning back toward the mews and his apartment on top. "I trust you're in good hands, though I'm not sure what to call him."

"It's still Mr. Walters," she reassured her driver. "Not a word of this to anyone, please."

Lady Matilda turned her attention to him. Walters swallowed. Anger darkened her blue eyes, and he longed to kiss it away, make her smile and laugh again. He took a seat next to her, his stomach aching as he bent forward. Nothing broken, but he'd be demmed sore tomorrow.

"I understand the position you are in," she began. "But I resent the charade. I want you to know that."

He nodded, wishing there was something he could say to make the situation better, more favorable.

"I also appreciate what you've done for me, outside of tonight."

His head jerked up, locking his gaze with hers. "I—"

She placed a finger on his mouth and shook her head. "I need to say this. Before I met you, I was terrified of meeting new people, especially men. It wasn't that I was frightened for my safety, but rather my reputation. Quiet people are often categorized as dull, which I'm not, of course. When I did speak, my nerves would increase, and I often stumbled, lending to the impression of being slow or simple."

Walters blew out a breath, not wanting to hear this lovely and kind woman had been wretched even for a moment.

"My mother was so forceful in her attempts to 'bring me out' that it had quite the opposite effect. She reinforced my insecurities, her endeavors convincing me I wasn't as good as the other girls." She chewed on her bottom lip, then looked up at him, eyes shining.

"My brother loved me unconditionally, of course. Mama was never the affectionate type. But since coming to know you, my angst has abated. I'm able to keep a conversation going without stumbling and not feel as though I shall spill my accounts." She smiled at him. A dazzling, heartbreaking smile that stole his breath. "Because of this, I have forged a better relationship with my mother. I realize she never saw me as inadequate but worried for my future, and I will face the upcoming Season with dread but not fear. And you are the reason for both of these miracles."

Walters snorted. "There is an inner strength in you that you haven't realized yet. There is more of your brother in you than you think." He stood, then reached out and took her hand, pulling her up with him. The hell with propriety when he only had minutes left with Lady Matilda.

"I hate to agree with you," she said, her voice trembling now, "but we cannot see each other again."

He nodded, his heart hurting with each breath. Her eyes were downcast, the lashes a crescent against her cheek. And then a tear escaped, tracking its way down her face. On instinct, he reached out and caught it with his finger.

Her hand flew to his, pressing his palm to her cheek. "Though I am grateful for all this, I will ask a favor of you before you walk out of my life."

His heart pounded fiercely. Could she hear it? How could he tell her that the uncertainty he took from her was internalized within him? The only time Walters did not feel sure of himself was with Lady Matilda. She put him off-kilter, muddled his mind, boiled his blood. No woman had ever affected him in this way. No woman ever would except for his—

"Mattie," he rasped, shocked her given name had slipped off his tongue. She still held his right hand, but the fingers of his left reached out to stroke her hair. He wanted to remember the silkiness of it, dream of her when he was alone, in the dark of the night.

"Kiss me, Harry," she whispered. "I need to know what it feels like to be kissed with sincere affection. I'm afraid I may never have the experience with anyone else."

"Then the men in your society are fools." Walters slid his

arm around her lower back and pulled her close. The contact, and the emotion of the moment, dulled the pain from his pummeling. His only thought was to make her happy.

He dipped his head and brushed her lips with his, the touch sending flames to his core. Unprepared for such a jarring sensation, he moaned against her mouth. He brushed her lips again, then pressed harder as her body melded into his. *Easy. Be gentle.*

But desire roared through him, and he pulled back, afraid his constraint would waver.

"You taste of honey and heaven," he whispered, leaning his forehead against hers. "I'm a lucky man to have sampled such a combination before I die."

"I was right, then? You do care for me?" Those ocean-blue orbs blinked up at him as if surprised at the revelation.

"If your brother wasn't an earl, or I had a title, there would be nothing that could keep me away from you... Mattie." He tossed out the guilt for using her pet name. This was a stolen moment, and he would pilfer every last second.

"I-I lov—"

His mouth covered hers, not letting her say the words that would haunt them both forever. This kiss was not gentle. It conveyed all the regret and love and despair in his soul. He kissed her, this one and only time, like a lover. Her arms went around his neck, and she pressed against him, and he silently cursed his body's instant reaction.

His tongue brushed the seam of her lips, and she opened them, giving him permission to explore. He slipped inside, fully tasting honey and heaven, knowing if his life were to end now, he would die a happy man. One hand cradled her face, the other moving up and down her back and over her hip. She whimpered against his mouth; her fingers twisted in his hair.

The sound of a door, a rustle of skirts. "My lady, your mother is still up, asking for you. I told her you were in the library," Miss Tilbot whisper-shouted from the kitchen.

Walters scanned Mattie's face, memorizing the high cheeks, the slight dent in her chin, the way her hair curled against her jaw. "You'd best find a mirror because right now you don't look like you've been reading."

Her chest rose and fell as she caught her breath. "What do I look like?"

"Like you've been thoroughly ravished." He tried to smooth the hair on top of her head. "You better go."

She nodded, still clinging to his neck. When she locked her gaze with his, she sucked in a deep breath. "Now I know."

With that, she picked up her skirt and ran into the house.

* * *

MATTIE STOPPED in the library to fetch a book and run up the stairs. She was breathless when she reached her mother's sitting room. "You wanted to see me?"

"Heavens, my dear, what happened to you?" Her mother's eyes were wide as she studied her daughter's disheveled appearance. "Do you have a fever? You're flushed."

Mattie shook her head. "I fell asleep in the library, mussing my hair. Then I ran up the stairs when Franny told me that you needed me." A twinge of guilt lit in her belly as she lied to her mother, but she certainly couldn't tell her the truth.

"I just wanted to tell you that the new dresses are completed. We need to make an appointment for the fitting."

"Any day good for you, Mama," she said. It didn't matter, for there would be no more outings with Mr. Walters to look forward to. She blinked back the hot tears. "Goodnight, then."

"Goodnight, sweet daughter," her mother murmured with a smile, then went back to her own book.

As soon as she'd left her mother's bedchamber, she ran to her room and slammed the door shut. And crumpled to the ground like an empty grain sack.

So this was love. Glorious, heart-wrenching, and hopeless. She sobbed for finding it. She sobbed for losing it. She sobbed for the fleeting happiness that had been so callously snatched away.

CHAPTER 12

Mid-November
Gracechurch Street

*T*he clan was gathered for Sunday dinner. They crowded into the parlor, laughing and talking over each other. It was like this every week. The patriarch handed out whisky to his sons while Maggie and Nora sipped sherry.

Walters looked around at his six siblings.

"Ye outdid yerself, my dear," Paddy called to his wife. "Yer stew always puts me back in Dublin, to be sure."

"'Tis why I make it," she said, beaming. "Nora, play us a song."

Honora took her seat at the harp, stretching her arms out and flexing her long, slender fingers. She pushed her mass of red hair over one shoulder and slid her hands up the strings, plucking a soft melody.

Walters watched his family as they discussed the past week. He wanted to share the information he gleaned, tell

Sampson what he'd learned, but now wasn't the time. Maggie's glare would shoot daggers at him if he brought up work after the Sunday meal.

Earlier in the month, he had followed two other men leaving the brothel after Colvin had gone home. When he'd followed them and realized one was Robert Dunn, a well-known thief who was as slippery as a greased pig, he'd heard them talking about a shipment. It had sounded as if they were stealing liquor from one brothel to sell it to another.

He had called in his brother, Gus Rutland, to accompany him on several clandestine outings, trailing the men to find out what they were up to. They learned Dunn had begun his criminal career at sixteen with an insurance scheme. Now, among other activities, he was making a profit from selling young boys. They had surveilled several flash houses, known for providing such services. It turned out Colvin had also become a patron of some of those same flash houses. Dunn was still working with a Spencean man, and Walters had seen both of them with Colvin in an alley behind one of the businesses.

He glanced at Gus, the second oldest, leaning against the mantel, as tall as Paddy but even brawnier. His hair was unfashionably long and tied back with a strip of leather. His dark-brown doe eyes were glued to Nora. It was a well-known secret that Gus fancied himself in love with Nora, who only loved *him* as a brother. The big blunderhead insisted she would see reason one day. To Nora's credit, she never gave him any hope that would happen.

Walters called out, "Nora, switch to the fiddle, and we'll sing a round of 'The Good-fellow's Resolution.'" This produced a chorus of approval.

Nora left the harp and, with the fiddle beneath her chin and a wide grin, laid the bow to the strings. Paddy belted out the first lines, tickling his wife beneath her chin.

Here in this Ballad you may see,
The vain-ness of bad Husbandry:
Good Advice here is to be found,
The which may save you many a Pound.

THE OTHERS BELLOWED out the next line, Aonarach joining with a long howl:

Drink t'other Bowl, I'le follow thee.

With a grin, Paddy continued,

I Have been a bad Husband this full fifteen year,
And have spent many pounds in good Ale, & strong beer
I have Ranted in Ale-houses day after day,
And wasted my time and my Money away:

But now i'le beware, and have a great care,
Left at the last Poverty falls to my share:
For now I will lay up my Money in store,
And I never will play the bad Husband no more.

AS THE REST of the men continued the verses, Paddy pulled his wife to her feet and swung her around the room in a lusty reel. He was surprisingly graceful, considering his size, and the couple moved as one. When the song finished, the audience of seven clapped heartily.

Maggie sat down, her hand on her heart, her chest rising

and falling with the exertion. "Oh my, Paddy luv, ye keep me young."

"Da longer to love ye, lass," he said, placing a loud kiss on her mouth.

Nora, Eli, and Ben groaned. Clayton and Sampson shook their heads.

"I t'ink I'm done for da night," announced Maggie. "It's been a wonderful evening, as always, but dere's work to be done tomorrow."

Ben, Eli, and Clayton decided it was also time to call it a night. The three, plus Sampson, had their own lodgings. Walters, Gus, and Nora still lived with the O'Briens. He supposed it was because the others had gone to university or another type of formal education and were used to living on their own. Eli had recently found his grandmother and now lived with her. Walters assumed they would all leave once they were caught in the parson's trap.

After everyone said their goodbyes to Maggie, Paddy turned to Walters. "Harry, ye've looked close to burstin' all night, so out with it."

Walters relayed the new information about Robert Dunn. "So, we can link Dunn to Sampson's parents, but we can also connect him to Colvin."

They all turned to Sam, whose neck had turned red, his face twisted in anger. "I don't care what we charge Dunn with, as long as we get him."

"And because Dunn was with one of the Spenceans, we may be able to link Colvin to the radicals." Paddy rubbed his pale-red stubble, the *scritch* loud in the silence as they all took in this information.

"From a legal perspective," offered Benjamin, the solicitor, "it's circumstantial but persuasive. We need a witness or statement to make it more concrete."

Eli, still working as a Runner, added, "If there is anything you need, let me know. I can pull information from Bow Street."

Walters nodded. "Gus has been helping since he finished his last case. I'll call in more help as needed." He paused, then let out a heavy sigh. "I may need Nora to play the strumpet."

Her smirk was contagious, and her brothers mirrored her expression. She looked at Paddy. "I'm not telling Ma. That's your job, Da."

"Aye, right. She won't like it, but I know yer brothers will keep ye safe," he said with a martyred expression. "And don't be looking so happy about playing a doxie."

Nora jumped up and hugged Paddy. "I promise not to like it too much, Da."

Paddy yawned. "I'm headed to bed myself. I'll leave da late nights to da young folk."

As soon as Paddy had taken the stairs, Nora turned to her brothers, her blue eyes bright. "Harry, what will you need me to do? Which part of Town so I know how garish to dress."

"I'll know more in a week. But I'm guessing it will be a flash house in the Dials. They've been taking the lads from White Chapel or Spitalfields and reselling them there," answered Walters. "We'll need you to melt into the crowd and find out where they're keeping the boys."

"I imagine they're chimney sweeps who grew too big and then sold to the highest bidder." Nora shook her head, glancing at Gus. "As if their lives weren't bad enough."

Gus patted her shoulder, a feral shine in his eyes. "Don't worry. We'll find them."

Walters hoped so. It was one of the wickedest trades in the city as his brother knew firsthand. Anything so lucrative was always hard to shut down.

* * *

LATE NOVEMBER
  Hanover Square

"MY OLD FRIEND Pendleton is coming to Town, and he has a sister your age," announced Nicholas at breakfast. "Mother, you remember the Pendletons?"

"Of course," his mother said. "I knew both his parents. How long will they be staying?"

"He'll only stay through mid-December or so. He wants to return to his wife as soon as possible." Nicholas turned to his sister. "I think you'll like Hannah. She'll be staying through the Season with a chaperone."

"It's not her mother?" asked Lady Darby.

He shook his head. "I'm not sure if she's ill or what the situation is, but someone else has been found. I thought it would be nice for Mattie to have a friend to whisper and giggle with at the balls and soirees."

"I do not whisper and giggle," Mattie retorted. "But I'm happy to meet her."

"Excellent. I'm sure he'll leave his card as soon as he arrives. His townhouse is in Berkeley."

"Perhaps he already has," said Lady Darby, sifting through the cards on the silver tray near her elbow. She took a sip of tea from her china cup, then handed a card to her son. "Here you are."

"Shall we have them for tea this week?" asked Mattie. If this were any of the ladies who had known her as a girl, she wouldn't be so excited. But here would be a chance for her to start with a clean slate, and she would do her best to make a new friend.

"That's a splendid idea," agreed her brother. "Mama, could you send round an invitation?"

"Of course."

* * *

TWO DAYS LATER, Mattie waited in the parlor for their guests. She pulled back the heavy curtain to see a gleaming black carriage with a gold crest on the side. The matching pair of bays snorted puffs of white into the chilly air as the tiger jumped from the back to open the door.

Rushing over to a wingback leather chair near the hearth, Mattie grabbed a book and plopped down as if she'd been there all morning. She stood as the butler announced the guests, smoothing the skirt of her pale-yellow wool skirt. A handsome man with brown hair streaked with gold entered, a plump older woman on his arm, and a beautiful young lady with dark honey-colored ringlets and amber eyes.

She wore a modest pale-rose day dress that did nothing to hide her generous figure. Puce Vandyke points of lace edged the square neckline and repeated in a double row at the calf and again along the hem. A satin ribbon matching the lace adorned the waist, with a redingote of the same color over the dress.

Mattie had a moment of panic when they locked eyes.

She's stunning. What will she think of me?

Then the girl smiled, and Mattie let out the breath she hadn't realized she'd been holding. Somehow, she knew they would be the best of friends.

In the hall, she heard Darby giving orders to the butler. "We will expect tea within the half hour. Lady Darby will not be attending us this afternoon. She has the megrim and is requesting chamomile tea in her room."

Fifteen minutes ago, the news that her mother wouldn't be there to help her navigate tea with strangers would have been upsetting, to say the least.

Nicholas entered the room. "Pendleton, it's good to see

you," he said, holding out his hand. The men shook and introductions were made.

Lord Pendleton's aunt, Lady Roberta, was the newly found sponsor and chaperone for Miss Hannah Pendleton. Mattie could see mischief in the older woman's eyes.

"It is a pleasure to meet any friends of my brother." Mattie was pleased to hear her voice sounded neither shy nor overly confident. "I apologize for my mother's absence." She gripped her book, spied her white knuckles clutching the spine, and loosened her hold.

"Is this by Maria Edgeworth?" asked Miss Pendleton, nodding at the book in Mattie's hand. "Have you read many of her books? I so enjoyed her novel, *Leanora*."

"Oh, yes. That's why I purchased *Castle Rackrent*. Have you read it?" Her mood brightened, and she smiled at her new friend.

"No, I haven't. Perhaps I could borrow it when you finish?"

"Oh, yes. Do you read any biographies?"

"Egad! Please don't tell me we have two bluestockings on our hands," Lord Pendleton said with a laugh.

"My sister has her nose in a book most of the time." Darby grinned. "She's indiscriminate and will read anything from a scientific journal to a romantic novel."

Mattie studied her brother as he spoke, watching his dimple deepen. *He likes her,* she thought. He seemed more animated than usual. His laugh not quite as deep as if he was—

Nervous! Nicky was flustered in front of Miss Pendleton?

She glanced at Lady Roberta, whose eyes were darting between her niece and Mattie's brother. She and Lady Roberta locked eyes. The older woman grinned, then winked at her. Mattie grinned back.

"Lud! This will be a delicious Season," said the matron. "Let's sit down and get to know one another, shall we?"

As Mattie served tea, they discussed upcoming public events and invitations that might be received in the future. Lady Roberta was in London often and kept in touch with many of those who enjoyed entertaining, listing those from whom she expected to receive calls and invites. "We will, of course, have several dinner parties at our townhouse." She took a sip of tea and added more cream. "I assume Lady Darby will also be arranging teas or possibly a ball? Your home is larger than ours, and I've seen the size of the ballroom upstairs."

"My mother spoke of planning a monthly event. I believe a musicale for February, a dinner for March, and perhaps a ball in April." Mattie offered the plate of small, crustless sandwiches and biscuits. "I must admit my nerves can get the better of me at times, though my mother assures me I will blend in with the others."

"Why would you want to do that?" asked Miss Pendleton. "I cannot wait for my first waltz. I've only been able to practice with my brother"—she gave Lord Pendleton an apologetic look—"and I can imagine what it's like..." Her voice drifted off as she focused on choosing a treat from the plate.

Mattie watched Nicholas's smile widen at the girl's easy distraction. She nibbled at a delicate fairy cake, her tongue darting out to catch the butter icing at the corner of her mouth. He opened his mouth to say something, then closed it. Was *he* struggling to make conversation?

"I would be honored to have your first waltz, Miss Pendleton," he said with a huge smile. It only faltered when the lady froze in mid bite at his words.

Miss Pendleton obviously hadn't expected his offer. She finished chewing and then cleared her throat. "That would be nice, indeed, Lord Darby."

Nicholas seemed confounded at her tone. Mattie hid her smirk. As a handsome, titled man, he was not used to a lady turning him down—even if only by her tone.

"I am accomplished in the waltz," he assured her. "I will not step on your toes or allow any mishaps." He gave her a smile that deepened the dimple on his cheek. When Miss Pendleton blushed, his confidence seemed to return. "It's settled then."

Lady Roberta flipped open her fan, her wrist moving back and forth rapidly. "Merciful heavens," she gushed, "this will be a monstrous good time."

Oh yes, Mattie decided, she liked these people immensely.

CHAPTER 13

First week of December
Almack's

The Pendletons had already invited them to dinner. Their aunt proved a marvelous hostess. She had arranged for parlor games which Lady Darby would never have dared to play. Mattie had been secretly happy when Mama had other plans that night. Spinning plates and blowing on feathers! It had been wonderful. To add to her happiness was her brother's attention to Miss Pendleton. Nicholas had offered to escort her before she'd even asked.

Could a romance bloom between them? Her brother deserved to find love, and if that woman was also her friend, even better.

Tonight, they were attending a ball, given by a friend of her mother's, who had graciously extended invitations to the Pendletons. Lady Darby was attending with them, explaining Almack's often rented out rooms, especially out of Season, and the patronesses were often invited to the event. "So you will most likely meet one or two of the patronesses tonight."

Mattie's stomach began to knot. She had been able to avoid Almack's at the end of last Season. Closing her eyes, she imagined herself standing next to Hannah—they were already using given names—and speaking with Mr. Walters. The image unraveled that nasty knot, and she drew in a deep breath. She wore one of her new dresses, a satin dress of umber with an overdress of Apollo gold lace. Thin gold ribbons were entwined in her hair, and a gold amulet hung from her ears and around her neck.

They entered the ground floor, and she rushed to Hannah's side. "Oh, you look lovely." Her friend wore a low-cut cream silk dress with a deep-violet flower print. A sheer cream overlay added a shimmer to her movements.

Hannah gave her a quick hug. "And so do you. I shall have to keep my distance, so you don't take all the attention."

"It's a draw," said Lady Roberta, then turned to Lady Darby. "It's good to see you again."

"Yes, the same," her mother said coldly, then nodded toward the stairs. "Shall we?"

Mattie squeezed Hannah's hand as they entered a large room, rectangular in shape, decorated with gilded columns. Ropes of red velvet designated an area for dancing. Chairs were placed along the outside of the room with mirrors covering the walls. Musicians warmed up on a balcony for the first dance set. During the Season, the dais was usually set up with chairs for the patronesses to watch the debutantes and invited guests.

One word from an Almack's patroness could ruin a debutante's hopes of a good match. These women also decided the dance partners for the young hopeful females on those Wednesday evenings. This was the place to mingle with the most eligible bachelors in Town. Lady Darby had already said there would be no problem getting invitations.

Now, it held the sponsor of the ball and their honored guest. Someone's brother who had been stationed in India and now returned to London. Lady Darby had explained it was a "reintroduction to society" of sorts.

* * *

THE ROOM WAS ALREADY FILLED with men in dark, tailed coats, trousers or breeches, and silk stockings, and of course the obligatory white cravat. It was the women who added color to the room. Every fashionable shade, in solid or print, could be seen in their gowns. Gems glittered under the gas-lit chandeliers: the earbobs on the ladies, tiaras, hair combs skillfully tucked within the elaborate hairstyles, and at the throats and fingers of both men and women.

"I see why the magazines call this the seventh heaven of the fashionable world," said Hannah, trying not to gape at the beau monde turned out for the ball.

Lady Darby took the lead, her silk gown of bottle green with an overdress of sheer black flowing behind her. "I feel like a newborn foal trailing after its mother," Hannah whispered as they moved in and out of the crowd, following the trembling feather on Lady Darby's green turban. She and Mattie walked arm in arm as Lady Roberta brought up the rear. Both men had disappeared.

Mattie watched as her mother stopped before a striking woman with dark hair, pink cheeks, and a rosebud mouth. "My dear Lady Cowper, I hoped you would be here tonight." Her mother sent a smug look toward Hannah's aunt. Nicholas had confided their mother thought the woman was less than refined. But did she have to be so rude?

"Ah, Lady Darby, so this is your lovely daughter." Lady

Cowper's shrewd blue eyes took in the small group. "I'm happy to welcome you, Lady Matilda."

"It's an honor, ma'am," Mattie said with a slight curtsy. "May I introduce—"

"Lady Roberta, is that you?" Lady Cowper beamed, her arms outstretched. "Where have you been hiding?"

Mattie's mother looked as though she might have an apoplexy, realizing the patroness was on such good terms with Hannah's aunt.

"You will have to tell me of your latest adventures, so I can relay all the information back to William," the patroness gushed, taking Lady Roberta's arm and giving it a squeeze. "And may I say the Devonshire brown really sets off your hair. I'm so glad you are not hiding those dark waves under a turban."

Lady Darby blanched, touching her own turban as Lady Cowper moved on. For the first time she could remember, Mattie felt sorry for her mother. Though the exchange had been a tit for tat, and her mother had deserved the subtle cut.

"What luck! The four most beautiful ladies in the room all in one spot. My search is over," Nicholas said as he joined them.

Mattie's confidence swelled as the evening progressed. Speaking with a group of people seemed natural with Hannah by her side. Lord Pendleton danced the first quadrille with her. Her second dance was with a gentleman Hannah had previously partnered with. Lord Smalley was a young baron, tall and lanky with a long face that Hannah said reminded her of a chestnut horse. When he smiled, his teeth were almost as large. But Mattie thought he had kind brown eyes, enjoying his sense of humor when he made fun of himself after stepping on her foot.

She and Hannah took a break from the dance floor, sipping lemonade and watching the crowd. Lady Roberta was talking to some friends, and her mother had gone to the necessary. She turned to see a dark-haired man on the other side of Hannah. He leaned in to say something in her friend's ear.

Hannah gave the man a side-glance and shook her head. "I'm afraid not. So we'll have to wait until formally introduced."

At that moment, Lord Smalley joined them. The dark stranger seemed to know him and introductions were soon made. When Mattie heard the name Duke of Colvin, the breath went out of her, and she grabbed Hannah's hand. She stared at the man who had caused the death of a young woman and so much grief for her brother.

He was handsome, in a cold way, but his raven eyes were cold, emotionless.

"My apologies, Lady Matilda," he said with a formal bow. "I did not realize who you were, or I would never have put you in such an awkward position." He turned back to Hannah. "It seems the son will always be punished for the sins of the father."

"I'm sorry to hear that Your Grace," Hannah murmured as she tucked Mattie's arm in hers. "If you'll excuse us—"

"He should be excusing himself," Darby interrupted. Mattie knew that tone, and fear twisted in her gut. "What the bloody devil do you think you're doing?" he hissed at the duke.

"As I told the *lovely* Miss Pendleton, I did not realize they were in your company. However, I do not think you have the authority to restrict where I go or who I converse with. Beware of your tone and remember who I am, Lord Darby." His black eyes glittered and a humorless smile curved his lips.

Her brother's jaw clenched, and Mattie knew he was thinking of the duke's past sins. As if they'd been summoned,

Lady Roberta and her mother appeared together, and the duke slipped into the crowd.

Much to her surprise, her brother did not demand they leave the premises. The baron found her later to apologize.

"I had no idea there was tension between the duke and your brother. I would never have taken it upon myself to introduce him. Please tell me that I am forgiven." His brown eyes pleaded with her, his body rigid as he awaited her answer.

She placed a hand on his arm to stop the movement and gave him a smile. "There is nothing to forgive, Lord Smalley. You have only acted the gentleman."

"Would it be too bold to ask if I may call on you?" His gaze landed on her eyes, then her mouth, then quickly darted to the floor, ceiling, and back to the floor.

Her heart went out to the man. He was nervous, and she understood the emotion. Mattie also liked him. Lord Smalley was not afraid to put his toe in the water, even if it was icy cold. In fact, his lack of good looks didn't put her off. She liked him more for it. Most handsome men were vain. If she were to spend her life with someone, Mattie wanted it to be a man she enjoyed being with, who would challenge her mind, laugh and debate with her. Harry's image flashed in her brain, and she pushed it back.

Mattie knew the only way to find out if he was such a person was to get to know him better. "Our at-home is on Thursday if you'd care to visit," she said in a tone she hoped sounded sincere. So she added, "I'm dreadfully thirsty. Would you mind getting me some refreshment?"

True joy lit his face, and Mattie was glad she had put forth the extra effort. After a promenade with the very chatty Lord Smalley, whose nervousness had now vanished, she danced twice more. Before dinner, Nicholas informed her they would be leaving.

"Of course," she agreed, "whatever you think is best."

She sought out Hannah to let her know they would not be staying for dinner.

"We are not staying either," Hannah told her. "Aunt Bertie has a dreadful headache, and in truth, I'm quite tired myself."

"Are we still going to Hatchards tomorrow?" Mattie asked her friend.

"Of course. I'll send a note to let you know what time we'll pick you up. Aunt Bertie has some other shopping to do. It should be a splendid afternoon, which could possibly end at Gunter's." Hannah hugged Mattie. "We'll talk more tomorrow about *that man*."

But when Mattie lay in her bed that night, the man who dominated her thoughts was not a baron or a duke. He was an investigator. And she fell asleep, dreaming of a waltz with Mr. Harry Walters.

* * *

WALTERS WAITED at The Guinea for Lord Darby. He had sent word this morning that he had new information. The earl had taken his advice and dressed as a working man whenever they met here. It was a tavern with a decent reputation where men came after a hard day's toil to have a bumper of ale and conversation, talk of high prices and low wages, who was getting married or having another babe, and enjoy a mutual camaraderie with others of their station.

He saw Darby enter in his brown wool coat and cap, looking like anything but a peer. His blond hair was mussed, sticking out from beneath the cap, and his jaw held a light layer of stubble. The earl had listened and followed Walters's advice.

He sat down and drank half the bumper that Walters had set in front of him. "He knows we're following him," Darby said straightaway. "He was at a ball I attended with my sister. He gained an introduction to them when he thought I wasn't looking."

Walters blinked. Colvin had been close to Lady Matilda? Rage poured through him, and it took all his willpower to keep his face bland. "Is your sister all right?" he asked in an even tone. He would skewer the duke, then place his head on a spike on Tower Bridge if Colvin had touched her.

Darby nodded. "Yes, but I think it shook her a bit. I'm not sure if he's watching her or Miss Pendleton—her brother is a close friend—and Colvin saw me dancing with her." The earl took in a deep breath. "He said Mattie wasn't his type, but Miss Pendleton was."

Walters let out a low whistle. "The Home Office is watching him too. Better he thinks it's us than the Crown. He won't hide from us. Let me tell you what I've learned."

Darby listened intently while Walters relayed the past week. The earl even smiled when Walters promised they were closing in on the duke. "He'll pay, my lord. Perhaps even more than you wanted."

"No punishment is too harsh for that man. He caught up with me while I was waiting for my carriage. Wondered if I had found out about *sweet Alice*." Darby pounded the table with his fist, causing a few patrons to turn and look. "*To the victor goes the spoils*, he said. As if this is just a game to him."

"I should have information on the flash house he is to visit. I wasn't planning on having you come along, but under the circumstances—"

"Yes," Darby cut in. "Send me word, and I'll be there."

Later that night, Walters walked off his frustrations. He wanted to go to Lady Matilda, *Mattie* as he'd begun to think of her. Was she fine, or keeping a brave face and petrified? If only he could hold her, look into those eyes the color of a summer sky, and hear her voice. Their kiss still haunted him.

When he finally stopped walking, he found himself in front of the Darby mews, looking up at the back of the dark townhouse. He hadn't set out with this destination in mind, but his thoughts had obviously brought him here.

What would Lord Darby do if Walters pounded on the door, demanding to see his sister? Grab a pistol and challenge him to a duel, most likely. He liked the earl, respected him, but Walters knew the boundaries and where the line was drawn.

CHAPTER 14

Mid-December
Seven Dials, St. Giles

olvin left his carriage, conferred with his toad waiting on a corner, and then both men continued on foot. Something wasn't right. The duke was making it easy—too easy. Besides the change from hackney to his own coach, there was an urgent air to him tonight. He followed the duke at a discreet distance, who followed his accomplice, and glanced across the street to be sure Darby was still there. Two ladies of the evening had tried to engage him, but the earl had deftly side-stepped them.

The duke's black cape and beaver hat faded into the misty night, only his silver cane tip flashing occasionally in the fog, like a tiny blinking beacon that kept their target within sight. The street narrowed; the local stores were dark now, the windows shuttered. As the buildings began to crowd together, taller structures bent against each other and tilted over the filthy streets and alleys.

Garishly clad women loitered against slimy walls, their attributes spilling out of their stained or frayed bodices, yellow smiles and crooked teeth flashing him as he kept a steady pace. A mangy dog scratched his ear, then scurried away from the kicks of a group of boys ambling down the street. A drunk stopped in front of him, tottering before he caught his balance, then pissed against the doorframe of a shop. This was St. Giles—a rookery, a slum.

The stench of rotting food, then human waste, grew more and more foul before Colvin turned into an alley. The toad, keeping a distance in front of the duke, stopped at a back entrance. He spoke with someone, then approached the duke, and they both entered the flash house.

Darby soon joined Walters in the shadows. "I'll go in, my lord, and see what he's up to. I have someone working on the inside, who may be able to gain access easier than me."

Walters hoped all was going well with Nora. But knowing Clayton was also inside gave him comfort. Gus had wanted to come, but the man was so big he'd attract attention. If anything ever happened to one of his siblings…

The Peelers and the Runners had informants in all the rookeries. When he was a Runner, he'd frequented these places, so he knew these streets and alleys well. He'd spoken with one of his old "acquaintances" who knew of Colvin's nighttime routine in this particular flash house.

The duke's visits were weekly. He asked for a private room and brought his own bottle. Then he would sit at a table and look over the young shirtless boys. He would send away any with scars or indications they'd been regularly beaten. Then choosing several, he would ask questions. His informant hadn't been able to hear what was asked because the duke spoke so softly.

Walters entered the tavern, smoke from the hearth filling the poorly ventilated room. The stench of unwashed bodies assaulted his nostrils. There were at least a dozen women working, two leading clients up the stairs to private rooms, others serving drinks. He spotted Clayton, singing with a trio of men, and his head ever so slightly nodded toward the opposite corner.

He followed the direction to see Nora, wearing a wig of white-blond curls and a low-cut red corset with sequins that caught the candlelight. She winked at a customer, who patted her arse, and she responded with a slap to his hand. The men at the table laughed, and she sashayed away.

Nora came up next to him, grinned at him, and patted his cheek. He bent close to her ear and said, "You're enjoying this too much."

She laughed, then bent over a nearby table to collect some empty bumpers for washing. "He's gone," she said in a sing-song voice. "In and out, just as quick as you please." She looked over her shoulder to make sure he'd heard and was satisfied with his nod.

"Get yourself out of here now. I'll let Pierce know we're done for tonight."

So his hunch had been right. The evening had been a ruse. To what end?

After a brief word as he passed by Clayton, he made his way out the back door to the alley. Turning the corner, he saw a man behind Darby, pointing a pistol at the earl's head. Walters pulled his own pistol and moved swiftly along the shadowed wall.

He smiled when the earl bent forward and then back with a *crack*. Head connected with head, and the footpad stumbled backward. Before Walters could assist, Darby threw a punch, catching the ruffian's jaw. The man was stunned but held firm. It took two more facers to set him to wobbling.

"Demmed stubborn rat," mumbled Walters, approaching the footpad from behind. He raised the butt of his pistol and brought it down on the man's crown.

"Colvin's gone. I think *this* was his purpose tonight." Walters nodded at the unconscious form and bent to pick up the ruffian's pistol. "I thought the sound of a shot might bring too much attention. What did he want?"

"A warning to leave off the duke. I milled his canister well enough before you fibbed him." Darby winced, rubbing the back of his head as he looked at the unconscious man. "I'm not complaining, mind you. I forgot how much that can hurt."

"I don't think we should linger here, my lord. Let's continue this conversation elsewhere." He tossed a grin over his shoulder and secured his weapon as they made their way out of the alley. "Preferably an establishment with decent ale."

They retraced their steps, out of the rookery, and to the hackney waiting for Darby. The earl beckoned him inside. When the driver moved forward, Darby took out a flask and handed it to Walters.

"He will go back to his old way, stalking gently bred ladies, if I continue my pursuit. I'm afraid his message is that he will go after my sister or Miss Pendleton."

Walters seethed inside, but he let out a whistle instead. "A noxious leech, ain't he?"

Darby grunted. "We need to remain diligent. I don't want any innocent victims, but I can't give up. This pustule on humanity must be stopped. Any suggestions?"

"Aye, and aye. First off, leave the rookery to me. If I set a new man on him, he may think he's scared you off." Walters chuckled. "He's just arrogant enough to believe it."

"While I hate leaving all the dirty work to you, it may be the safest plan to keep the ladies out of danger."

"We're making him nervous if he's resorting to threats. Good sign, I think." The cab rolled to a stop in front of the Guinea, and Walters stepped out.

"Thank you for your help. You have been indispensable." Darby held out his hand, and Walters shook it.

"Think nothing of it, my lord. I'll keep in touch in the usual fashion."

* * *

WALTERS STOOD AGAIN in the shadows behind Darby's house, leaning against a corner of the mews. He shouldn't be here. It was his third time this week. The threat of Colvin even considering harm to those under Darby's protection chilled him to the bone. And tore at his heart.

Mattie was in there somewhere, behind those cold stone walls. Did she think of him? Did she hate him? Would he ever have the chance to speak to her again, see the excitement in her sky-blue eyes, hear the lilt of her voice as she said his name, or touch the silky flaxen tresses? No. He needed to push her from his mind. An impossible feat. She was made to be remembered, adored, cherished.

* * *

MATTIE STOOD at the side of her window, peeking behind the curtain. She should be in bed, but she couldn't sleep. Couldn't close her eyes knowing he was down there. Her heart screamed to run to him, throw her arms around him, tell him it made no difference who his parents were or where he was born.

It would be folly. They were doing the right thing, what was expected of them, though no one knew their secret. No one who could impose a censure or punishment. Besides, she and Harry—it's what she called him in her dreams—were both paying the consequences already. They were apart.

Would she ever hear his laugh again? Feel the heat rush through her when those dark-chocolate eyes hungrily scanned her face?

She loved him, and he had ruined her for other men. Instead, Mattie would choose someone she liked, whom she could be friends with, and try to find a way to be happy. As she had the last two times he'd kept watch over her, she blew him a kiss that he would never feel.

When he pushed away from the stable and disappeared down the alley, a piece of her heart went with him. If he kept these vigils, she would have no heart left at all.

CHAPTER 15

Next night
Gracechurch Street

*W*alters entered the entry hall, wanting nothing more than a quick whiskey and a warm bed. He had an appointment to report to Lord Chester the next day. Nora had located the room where the stolen boys were kept in the last flash house. The duke had returned later in the week, browsing a potential purchase.

Clayton had overheard Colvin making arrangements for payment and "delivery" of his purchase. He, Clayton, and Gus had returned and taken the boys just before dawn. He would have loved to see the surprise and rage when the lads were discovered missing.

Bow Street was taking over this part of the investigation, and Robert Dunn and his Spencean friend must have gotten wind of the Runners. Neither could be found right now. As a previous Runner, Walters knew the constables would stay on the case until the men reappeared, either in Town or floating in the Thames.

Had their boss, "the Vicar," murdered them to keep their mouths shut? *Who was he?* Obviously not a man of God. And why the nickname?

George Edwards, the spy within the radical group, had also been pushing his friendship with the leader, Arthur Thistlewood. He'd discovered the address of a warehouse used to hold the weapons supply, bought by the money passed on by Colvin. Edwards had also discovered the name of the lad who took the money from Colvin.

With Clayton's help, they'd discovered the boy was the son of a Spencean. The one who had been stealing and selling to flash houses with Dunn, who seemed to have his thumb in too many pies.

Halfway up the stairs, a voice called out, "'Tis about time ye returned home. Almost drank all da whisky without ye," declared Paddy from the doorway of the parlor. "We'd have a word if ye please, Harry."

Walters frowned. *We?*

Lord Chester Hatford from the Home Office sat before the hearth, smiling as Walters joined them. "Take a seat, Mr. Walters. I have good news."

"Are my services no longer needed?" he asked.

"Quite the opposite. First, tell me what you've learned since we last spoke."

Walters did, bending to give Aonarach a scratch, then leaned back to enjoy the amber liquid provided by Paddy. "Is there enough to charge Colvin with something?" He blew out a breath. "Anything?"

Lord Chester grinned. "I'll tell you what I've been doing now." He held out his glass to Paddy, who took it to the side table and refilled his at the same time.

"The Spencean you saw with Dunn is in our custody now.

Conveniently, an unidentified body was found in the Thames, who is now known to be the disappeared radical."

"And his boy? The one who acts as the pickup?" Walters hated the lad going to prison for doing as his father bid.

"No, he's with his mother, who believes her husband is in hiding. It's the only way to ensure his safety until the trial. We know the man financing the radicals is called *The Vicar*."

"I heard Dunn mention the name Vicar. Who is he?" Walters had a feeling this fellow had a few irons in the fire.

"We don't know. Those we've brought in or arrested who worked for him have never met him. Only his moniker is used. Whoever his top men are must be extremely loyal or extremely afraid of him."

"But he's in Town?" Paddy asked.

Lord Chester nodded before changing the subject to ask Paddy, "Did you ask the missus about your daughter helping us?"

Paddy nodded. "I asked before I presented it to Nora. My daughter's response was never in question."

"Perhaps I've missed some *tiny* detail?" asked Walters, wondering how Nora came into this picture.

"We have enough evidence to charge the Duke of Colvin with treason. However, he seems to have a virtual army within his house, hired for his protection. I believe if we were to arrest him at the house, there would be resistance. He might even have an escape route prepared in case he's caught." Lord Chester shook his head. "The deviant is sinking into the depths of Hell."

"As if he could go much lower." Paddy loved sarcasm. He ran a hand through his faded red hair. "He'll take the bait for the dance, though. It's a brilliant plan, Hatford."

Lord Chester nodded, looking pleased by the compliment. "There is a masquerade at the end of the week, given by a, shall we say, *mutual friend*? Darby will be there, along with his sister and her friend the duke commented on. We made sure Colvin received an invitation and a whisper in his ear about the other guests."

Walters whistled. "Clever. You're right. He'll take the bait. So, what does this have to do with me and Nora?"

"You will both be going to the masquerade," said Lord Chester. "We'll arrest him during the event, where his minions can't protect him. Nora will make sure he remains *occupied*. And then lead him to a designated area where we will be waiting."

"I don't t'ink I've seen ye smile in weeks, Harry," said Paddy. "Finally, some good news, eh?"

Walters nodded. "If anyone can charm Colvin, it would be our Nora. But why do you need me? Won't you have your own men?"

"Of course, but you would recognize anyone who shouldn't be there—any of his henchmen—or a Spencean who could warn him of our presence."

It was true. Walters had been surveilling the Cato Street loft and knew all the faces of the members, along with the duke's toads. "How will I present myself?"

Paddy slapped him on the shoulder and guffawed. "It's a masquerade, boyo."

* * *

"Good morning, Brother dear." Nora entered the dining room with a wide smile on her face. "I hear we will be working together again."

Walters shook his head. "Again, you are much too cheerful, considering you must entertain a man who sold his soul to the devil."

"It's just another role on a different type of stage," she retorted. "I've been thinking about our costumes."

Walters leaned against the back of the chair. "Please, Lord, save me from the machinations of my sweet sister."

Nora laughed. "I think you will like your costume. A pirate. You shall go by the name of Jack Rackham."

"Calico Jack." He brightened. "The good man turned terror of the seas."

She nodded. "It will provide enough cover so your face won't be easily recognized, and the costume will be comfortable enough you can chase or wrestle with the villain if need be."

"And who will you be?"

"A concubine with a veil over my face," she said, her eyes daring him to argue.

Walters shook his head. "Don't let Maggie see you in that deuced costume if it's the same one you wore for the Ali Baba production. She still has hopes for a respectable daughter."

* * *

MATTIE CLAPPED HER HANDS. "Oh yes, it's perfect!"

She was at the dressmaker's with her mother and Hannah. Hannah's costume for the following evening was Eleanor of Aquitaine. She would wear a forest-green medieval gown with a black silk underdress and a black velvet rope to drape low across her waist. A string of holly and mistletoe had been embroidered across the dark hem and along the black lace armbands, cuffs, and neckline.

Mattie twirled in front of the mirror, inspecting her traditional Venetian costume. The black hooded cape covered a coquelicot gown with white poppies embroidered in stripes down a full red skirt. Her mask was red with a border of black paste diamonds, and it made her light blue eyes stand out against the darker color. "It's beautiful."

"You're beautiful, Mattie," whispered Hannah in her ear.

"You are both beautiful," agreed Lady Darby. "I understand Lord Smalley will be there."

"He didn't mention it when we saw him at the soiree last week." The baron was beginning to feel like a favorite armchair. Comfortable. She would not think about how her heart didn't pound when she thought of him. Would she ever be kissed again like Harry had kissed her? *Move on.*

While her mother arranged to have the outfits delivered to their individual directions, Hannah tugged on Mattie's sleeve.

"Will your brother be attending?"

Mattie shrugged. "I don't know. This time of year he's always hit with a bout of the blue devils. But I will try to convince him."

"I have heard masquerades can be dens of iniquity," said Hannah, a mischievous gleam in her eye. "We could receive a kiss from a stranger."

"And do you have a particular stranger in mind?" Mattie thought if she couldn't have the man of her heart, perhaps her friend could. How wonderful it would be to have Hannah as a sister. *A sister.* The thought made her want to squeal with delight.

"What about you? A handsome masked man could sweep you off your feet as well."

Mattie forced a smile. *Only if he comes out of my dreams, I'm afraid.*

And goodness, there had been enough of those.

CHAPTER 16

The masquerade ball

*W*alters was almost giddy. Tonight they would arrest Colvin. One case would come to an end. With the information the duke would provide, the second case might soon be completed.

He checked the mirror, tugged on his beard to make sure it would stay in place, then added the eye patch and a worn tri-cornered hat. A cloth tied around his head held the two shoulder-length braids in place. His long red coat included a sash for the sword on his hip and large blue cuffs covered his wrists. His breeches tucked into tall leather boots.

"You make a handsome pirate, Brother," said Nora from the hall, opening her cloak to reveal her costume.

"I look ridiculous, but the costume does its purpose." Walters chuckled. "Keep that cape closed and pull up the hood. If Maggie sees you, she'll lock you in your room."

Nora's silk turquoise pantaloons did nothing to hide her

figure. Beneath the sparkling bodice of the same color, she wore a shirt of sheer flesh-colored material, giving the illusion her stomach and arms were bare. Her veil was secured with a band embellished with turquoise stones. Her brilliant red hair spilled down her back, barely contained by the veil.

When they arrived at the townhouse on the Strand, there was a line of carriages waiting. The front of the brick house was bathed in light, uniformed footmen holding open the double-wide doors. Nora put a hand on his arm when he moved to exit the coach. Walters wanted to get out and walk; he hated wasting time.

"Harry, a member of the *ton* would wait patiently until we arrived at the portico. Remember you are not a working man tonight," Nora said softly. "We will be there soon enough."

His shoe tapped on the floor, and then his sister placed a hand on his knee to keep it from bobbing. "I love you, Brother, but you are driving me mad."

This delay was making *him* mad. Finally, Roger Lynch appeared at the window, signaling it was time to alight. The boy stood proud in his dark livery, keeping a serious face as he extended his hand to assist Nora. She gave the lad a smile that sent a blush rushing up his neck and face.

Walters took his sister's arm and hurried up the portico steps, remembering not to acknowledge the wall of footmen. They walked up a circular staircase to the next floor. When they reached the grand ballroom, his jaw almost dropped. He'd never attended a *ton* event before, and the amount of money in this room, the three gas-lit chandeliers, wall hangings, and costumes, was astounding. The collection of satin and silk, masks, jewels, fobs, and canes was a dazzling display of glitter and pomp. He thought of his humble beginnings and wondered how long one diamond ear bob would have fed him as a child. How well Roger Lynch's family could live on its proceeds.

"How are you not amazed at this show of wealth?" he asked Nora.

"I'm an actress. I live in a pretend world much of the time, and this is just another set of props." Nora moved through the guests as if she belonged there, nodding her head at various people as she passed.

"Do you know them?" Walters wouldn't be surprised.

"Of course not, Harry. But they don't know that. It's a *masquerade*." Nora moved toward a pair of French doors. "Let's find a spot with a breeze. It may be December, but it's horribly warm in here."

There were several pirates in the throng, one also in a red coat. Good. Darby would be dressed as Casanova, which Walters thought amusing. His sister would be dressed in a Venetian cape with a hood, and her friend would attend as Eleanor of Aquitaine. It would be easier to spot Darby if he were with the two ladies.

His eyes scanned the room, darting from sultans wearing large turbans, several bishops, a few monks, and—

Walters knew it was Lady Matilda before she turned to face him. Her presence was like a finely spun spider's web: Once caught, it was impossible to escape the silken threads. She joined an older woman in a blue sari painted with tiny birds of paradise. Mattie leaned forward and gave the medieval-looking woman a quick hug.

Miss Pendleton and her aunt, he thought.

Beneath her cape was a gown of red with some fancy embroidery. Her red mask had a black border with diamonds that made her clear blue eyes stand out. His heart leapt. He wanted to run to her, pick her up, and swing her in a circle above his head. Let her laughter flow over him. Instead, he dragged his eyes from the vision of perfection and continued to search for Darby.

A quarter hour later, a man in a brown wig, pulled back

in a short tail, and azure satin breeches took a place beside him. A long gold coat partially covered his white shirt with ruffles at the neck and sleeves. And familiar blue eyes.

"Everything in place?" Darby asked, his eyes straight ahead.

Walters nodded and did the same, not making eye contact. "On my other side is the lady who will be entertaining the duke." Nora gave Darby a quick glance, then began to mingle. "The constable and his men will be waiting at the designated place at half past eleven. This will be over by midnight."

"I already spotted Hatford. He has informed his superiors, who will be waiting for word of the arrest." Darby's foot tapped. "Is there anything I can do?"

"My lord, in order to maintain the persona, I may need to *dance*." The word came out as a grimace. "Do I have your permission to ask one of the ladies with you tonight? It would be easier than asking a stranger who might realize I don't belong here."

"That would be fine."

"Then let us begin the chase."

Darby let out a long sigh. "I've waited too long for this night."

"Good hunting." Walters followed Nora into the sea of guests.

MATTIE WAS DISAPPOINTED her mother hadn't attended, and Lord Pendleton had returned to his country estate to attend his wife and mother. But her brother had filled the void, dressed as the dashing Casanova. She secretly hoped he would whisk Hannah away and kiss her in some dark corner.

"I see someone I need to speak with," Darby murmured in her ear. "Can I escort you somewhere first?"

Her eyes landed on her friend. "No, I see Hannah and Lady Roberta. Join us later?" At his silence, she glanced up at him. His eyes were pinned on Miss Pendleton, an expression on his face she had rarely seen these past years. Happiness? Anticipation? Both, she hoped.

Mattie made her way to her friends, passing two wizards, a couple of servants, and some sort of goddess.

"Welcome, my ladies," she said in an atrocious Italian accent, trying not to giggle. "I am a stranger here in England and in need of friends."

The three laughed, and she leaned in to give her friend a quick hug. "You look stunning," she told Hannah.

"You'd think you girls have been friends since childhood," added Lady Roberta. "How did you know it was us, my dear? Are we so apparent?"

Mattie laughed. "Well, I've already seen Hannah's costume, and you said you would wear something from your travels. And as I got closer, I could hear your voice. It is quite distinct, Lady Roberta."

The older woman chuckled. "Well played! Now, let's mingle and see who is who, shall we?"

They moved slowly to the other side of the room, where they waylaid a footman with a tray of wine glasses. As they sipped champagne and observed the crowd, Hannah's brows drew together. "Why does that sailor look so... feminine, and that queen so... uncomely?"

"Oh my dear, I forgot this is your first masquerade," explained Lady Roberta. "Women dress as men, men dress as women. All the more difficult to decipher who is behind the mask. It is monstrous funny, is it not?"

"Nicholas is here somewhere. He had to speak with someone and promised to join us soon." Mattie searched the room. "I pointed you both out to him when we entered. He said to give you his regards, and he'll join us shortly."

Hannah's face dropped. Mattie's arm looped arms with her friend. "If you could only have seen his face when he saw you. His mouth fell open."

Lady Roberta grinned. "Of course it did. And I'm sure you've dropped a few jaws yourself this evening, Lady Matilda."

As the orchestra was warming up, Darby found them. He whispered something in Hannah's ear that made her smile, then blush. He bowed and kissed her gloved knuckles, then did the same with Lady Roberta. She assumed he would ask Hannah to dance. Without Lord Pendleton to ask for her first dance, as had become their custom, her eyes searched the room for anyone who appeared familiar. Was Lord Smalley in attendance? She hadn't asked when he'd visited last week, and the baron hadn't mentioned it.

A pirate approached her and bowed. She blinked, then shivered. He bent before her, and the long umber braids swung with the movement. When he straightened, his dark eyes twinkling, her breath hitched. His long red coat stretched across his broad shoulders, the tight breeches revealing the muscular thighs.

Do not swoon.

"Madame," Mr. Walters asked, "may I have this dance?"

She glanced at her group, then smiled. "Why, good sir, I cannot dance with a stranger, let alone a treacherous pirate. My brother would never allow it."

"I am John Rackham at your service, ma'am." He put his hand to the side of his mouth and whispered loudly, "Known to some as Calico Jack."

All three ladies gasped in mock horror, enjoying the theatrics.

"I've always wanted to dance with a pirate," Mattie

answered, hoping her hands did not tremble when she took his arm. "But you must promise not to kidnap me, for I have to be home by dawn."

"I cannot vouch for my honesty, but chivalry is not dead, my lady." He held out his arm as the first notes of a quadrille began.

"If I am not back by the end of the set, send out the Royal Navy," called Mattie over her shoulder. Nicholas was studying Mr. Walters, a peculiar expression on his face. She grinned up at the handsome pirate, her heart racing. How many times had she dreamt of this moment? Yet, the fact he asked her to dance gave her courage.

"It's the strangest thing, but you remind me of someone," she said, batting her eyelashes. She hoped she looked like a coquette and not like she had something in her eye.

"As do you," he said, his deep baritone making her warm all over. "Anyone in particular?"

"Yes, a strange man who watches our house at night. Lately, even when my brother is home."

Mr. Walters stopped, coughed, then began moving them forward again. "I-I don't have a good explanation. I hope tonight will end the need for it."

Disappointment poked her chest. "Oh, I see. It was a necessity?"

He paused and locked eyes with her. "Like breathing."

Her pulse raced, and she saw his gaze linger at her neck. Then another thought occurred to her. *Of course!* "You are close to catching the lickpenny?"

Mr. Walters nodded as they joined the line of dancers for the quadrille. "I needed to share the moment with someone who would understand."

Her heart soared with this unexpected encounter and the secret *Harry* had just divulged. How could she think of him as anything but *Harry* when he was so close?

As they met one another in the center of the line, hands out, palms touching, she asked, "How do you know the dance?"

They separated and came together again. "My sister taught me. However, I'm a clumsy ox, so please look out for your toes and keep me from making a fool of myself."

The dance progressed, and each time they came together, bodies close, hands touching, she fell a little more in love with him. His signature scent of orange and leather also invaded her dreams. Everything about this man haunted her.

When the quadrille ended, she took his arm. He bent low and whispered in her ear, "I must leave you now. Be awake on all suits tonight. He is here, and I don't know what he may try. But I worry he will attempt to get close to you or your friend."

Bile rose in her throat at the thought of the Duke of Colvin touching her or Hannah. He returned her to Lady Roberta, who nodded toward the dancers lining up for the next set. Nicholas was partnering with Hannah. They both appeared smitten by the looks they gave each other. That cheered Mattie, and she pushed the duke from her mind.

CHAPTER 17

"*I* can't find him," said Nora in a rush, standing on her tiptoes to peer over the crowd again.

"What?" He tried to keep the irritation from his voice.

"He went to relieve himself, and he hasn't returned. Darby is still here, but only two of the women."

He followed her line of sight and saw Lady Roberta and Lady Matilda. Relief swept through him, but only for a moment. "I'll talk to the ladies and find out where Miss Pendleton is."

Walters drew in a deep breath and made himself walk at a leisurely pace when he wanted to shove the people out of his way.

"Your handsome pirate has returned, Lady Matilda."

Mattie's smile faded when he shook his head.

"What has happened?"

"Where is your friend?" His voice remained low but urgent. He had to find the duke.

"She went to use the—"

"We were just asking ourselves the same thing," Lady Roberta interrupted. "She's been gone too long."

Lady Matilda gasped. "Lady Roberta, remember the high-wayman who came past us earlier, and he bumped into her?"

"It didn't seem like an accident," added the older woman, a glint of anger in her eyes.

"Something about him was familiar. His eyes, those cold black eyes. It was the duke!" A slender hand covered her mouth. "Oh, Harry," she cried. "Please find her. I will find my brother and send him to help."

Walters nodded. "Tell him I will meet him on the ground floor."

By the time he'd made a sweep of the top level and reached the ground level, he found Darby striding toward the stairs. "We need to check this floor and below."

"I'll head below," Darby said. "I know this house. I'll take the servants' stairs. Meet me when you've finished."

The earl disappeared down the corridor just as Nora entered the entryway. "What can I do? I saw you talking to the ladies."

"They aren't here. Check with the footmen and make sure they haven't left. Then fetch Lady Matilda and the other woman. I'm joining Darby in the cellar." He patted his side for reassurance, the pistols stored in his belt giving him comfort.

Walters finished searching the ground level, then took the servants' stairs. He moved down the dark hallway, hearing voices on the left, then shouts. Rushing to the open door, he found Darby on top of the duke, pummeling his face and head. The earl was in a rage and had lost all sense until Lord Chester, who stood in the shadows, announced, "Darby! If you kill him, we can't hang him."

This seemed to restore the earl's reasoning. He still strad-dled Colvin, but his arms hung by his sides, his breath coming in heavy pants. "I'd prefer to do it myself," he argued, wiping the sweat from his face with his coat sleeve.

The duke turned his head to the side and spit. Vile laughter faded into a bout of wheezing. "Look at the note. It's signed with a *C* for Colvin." He spit again and drew in a harsh breath. "She met me willingly. And even if she didn't, I would never hang for rape. I am the sixth Duke of Colvin, and my father served the King well."

The disgusting man was trying to ruin the reputation of a lovely, innocent woman. Walters fists bunched, wanting to feel his own knuckles crunch into the man's arrogant face.

"I thought it was *C* for Casanova." Miss Pendleton's voice was no more than a croak. "He trapped me in here, i-in the dark."

"Tell that to a jury of my peers." Colvin tried to push Nicholas off, let out a low moan, and fell back against the flagstone. "No matter what you accuse me of, I'll cry off with privilege of peerage."

Walters stepped back as the constable and one of his men approached the room and entered. He saw the smirk on Lord Chester's face as he stepped from the shadows and nodded toward the duke.

Darby moved to help Miss Pendleton up and swept her into his arms. The duke yelled at the men pulling him from the floor. "Do not touch me, you blasted imbeciles. I am a Peer of the Realm! I am above this, I say!"

The men ignored his tirade and jerked him to his feet, stopping before Lord Chester. "I'm afraid your privileges do not extend to treason, my lord. I'm sure your father who, as you pointed out, was a loyal subject of the King, would agree. I suggest, if you wish to retain any dignity, you should come with us quietly."

"Who the bloody hell are you?" he asked, spitting more blood as the first tinge of fear coated his words. "I demand to speak to someone with authority."

"That would be me, Lord Chester Hatford. I am a representative of the Home Office and the Crown. We have been watching you, Your Grace. It seems you have interesting friends who ask you for money." Lord Chester placed himself in front of the battered duke. "Unfortunately, it's those investments which seem to have caused the Crown some anxiety."

"*You've* been watch—There has been some mistake." Walters watched the duke's face pale as he realized Darby had not been the real threat. "Y-you have no proof of wrongdoing."

"Ah, but we have, or I would never presume to put you, the Duke of Colvin, under arrest. I'm afraid your rendezvous with the Cato Street radicals have been documented, along with your funding of the Spencean Philanthropists." He shook his finger at the duke. "Your Grace, consorting with factions who wish to overthrow our government is high treason. Shameful, really."

"I demand—"

"I am sorry, but you are not in a position to demand. Your only hope will be to share names. Names of those plotting to assassinate our cabinet, names of the conspirators who believe it is permissible to overthrow our government. We'll be sure to provide you pen and paper in the Tower, so you can write down everything. Perhaps then, the Regent will reduce the hanging and quartering to a beheading." Hatford gave a mirthless chuckle. "I've been told it's much quicker and more humane. And I understand from your friend Lord Darby that you are quite the humanitarian."

Walters heard more voices and turned to find Nora, Lady Roberta, and Lady Matilda descending the stairs.

Darby was carrying out Miss Pendleton. "Walters, make sure they get home safely, will you?"

"Of course. The physician will be sent to your home."

Lady Roberta pushed past Walters to follow her niece and

bumped into Hatford. "Let me see my niece... Chester! Merciful heavens, is that you?"

"Bertie?" Hatford asked. "My Bertie from Calcutta?" He beamed. "The young lady is fine. Come along with me."

The two began chatting as if they'd run into each other at Gunter's. Lord Chester led the way to a waiting coach at the back of the house, and Walters stopped Lady Matilda from following. "Lord Darby requested I see you home."

Her azure eyes flicked from his face, to her brother's retreating back, and returned to him.

"She will be fine." He lifted his hand to rub her arm, give her some comfort, when she threw herself against his chest, clinging to him. The sobs began, and he held her, rocking her back and forth, stroking her hair. "*Shh*, it's over."

Nora stood on the stairs. "I'll have Mr. Lynch bring the carriage round."

"Send him this way. I don't want Lady Matilda to be seen like this."

IN THE CARRIAGE, he sat next to Mattie, tossing propriety to the dogs. He held her close until she blew her nose and dried her tears with her handkerchief.

"Thank you."

"I was only doing my job."

Lady Matilda shook her head. "You're a good man, Harry."

She stared at Nora, sitting on the opposite bench. "And thank you, Miss..."

"O'Brien. Nora O'Brien. I'm Harry's sister." She reached out her hand and the two women shook. "Meeting you makes some things going on with my brother much clearer."

"The actress."

Walters glared at his sister, who smirked back. "And you are correct. My brother is the very best of men."

When they stopped in front of the Berkeley Square house, Walters helped her out. She stretched on her toes and placed a kiss on his mouth, tears still shining in her eyes. "I love you, Harry Walters. Don't ever think otherwise. And I would give up anything to be with you."

Then she picked up her skirts and ran up the portico and into the house.

When he climbed back into the coach, he avoided Nora's eyes.

"When were you going to tell us that you've fallen in love?" she asked, her voice soft, not even a trace of humor.

"Our affection cannot grow, so it is a moot point." He crossed his arms, wishing he could stop at the Dog's Bone for a drink to celebrate the duke's arrest. And forget Mattie. But he could see the grin on Leo's face when he ordered an ale. No, he'd already made a fool himself in front of Lady Matilda. He couldn't endure more teasing.

"She loves you."

"It's not enough," he said irritably. "We're too different."

"You're in a different class not a different world. Love is always enough if it's sincere and strong enough."

"You're naïve, Sister."

If there was a way, Harry would have found it. How many nights had he racked his brain to find one?

CHAPTER 18

Late January 1820
Hanover Square

"*I*'m so happy for you," Mattie exclaimed. "I can't believe the banns are being read, and we will soon be sisters!"

Hannah pulled Mattie onto the settee. "You will stand up with me, won't you?"

"Of course." Mattie beamed. She was happy for both her brother and sister-to-be.

"And you will be a bride by the end of the Season," teased Hannah. "I feel it in my bones, as our estate manager likes to say."

Mattie studied the toes of her slippers and clamped her lips together. She would not spoil their joy. It had taken five years for Nicholas to recover from his first marriage. To think he found retribution and love in the same month was almost a miracle.

"If you think you are hiding anything from me, you can stop the ruse. What is the matter? You haven't been right in weeks." Hannah's amber eyes narrowed. "Did Lord Smalley say something? Did you have words?"

"No! He's a dear man, really. A… friend." Mattie sighed.

"That doesn't sound hopeful."

They both sat in silence for a bit until Lady Roberta entered and rang for tea. "What's come over the two of you?"

"Mattie is unhappy."

"No, I'm not. I am thrilled about the wedding. It's not that."

Lady Roberta took the wingback chair, sitting across for the girls on the chaise longue. "It's the pirate, isn't it?"

"What pirate?" Hannah's brows drew together, then she gasped. "The one you danced with at the masquerade?"

Mattie was mortified, her face growing hot.

"Aunt Bertie always knows these things. You might as well tell us the whole story, for we won't leave you alone until you do."

"Indeed, my girl. You'll feel much better once you get it off your chest."

Once Mattie opened her mouth, the words spilled out. After two pots of tea, she finally finished.

"How romantic," breathed Lady Roberta.

"We have to find a way for you to be together," said Hannah, now on her feet and pacing. "There must be something we can do."

Mattie shrugged. "Mama would have an apoplexy. And Harry"—she let out a little smile at the use of his given name—"would never propose because of his lack of title."

"So, he wouldn't elope?" When Mattie shook her head, Hannah began pacing again. "Have you spoken of this to your brother?"

"Nicky can't provide him with a title."

Lady Roberta crossed her arms. "Do *you* care about titles?"

"Not at all," Mattie blurted.

"Does he love you?"

She blinked at Lady Roberta's question. "Yes." Deep in her heart, she knew it was true.

"I think you should tell Lord Darby how you feel," the older woman said, tapping her bottom lip with a finger. "Fate always puts people together for a reason."

"I agree." Hannah hugged her. "Aunt Bertie and I will do everything in our power to make this right."

"Don't give up hope, my dear," Lady Roberta advised. "Love will wait as long as it must if two people are willing."

"Like you and Lord Chester?" asked Mattie with a sly grin.

"Exactly." The older lady waggled her brows. "Let's just hope you aren't my age by the time we arrange it."

* * *

EARLY FEBRUARY
Gracechurch Street

"THE VICAR AGAIN?" mumbled Walters. "Colvin has no idea who the blaggard is?"

Lord Chester shook his head. "He would tell if he did. The man is facing the noose."

"And we haven't found Robert Dunn yet." Walters drummed his fingers on the table. They were sitting in the O'Briens' parlor, sipping a fine French brandy. A gift from Hatford. "Except for Thistlewood, most of the Spenceans are growing suspicious of your spy. Edwards is getting nervous."

"I don't blame him. His notes say the men are concerned

because the funds have dried up. I need you to get him some blunt and curb the unease in the group."

"I can do that. But what's the plan?"

"It involves a bit of trickery." Lord Chester gave Paddy a side-glance.

"Ye're checking with an Irishman about trickery?" The big man guffawed. "Let's hear it."

"We'll plant an article in one of the newspapers. Thistle-wood reads the *New Times,* I think Edwards said. It will mention the cabinet is meeting at Lord Harrowby's house for a dinner and cabinet meeting. He lives around the corner in Grosvenor Square, not far from the Cato Street meeting place."

Walters let out a whistle. "We'll lure them into committing a crime?"

"If you have a better plan, I'm open," said Lord Chester.

"So, Edwards will make sure they see the post?" Paddy asked.

"Yes, and he'll suggest hitting the entire cabinet at once."

"It could work," agreed Walters. "I wouldn't leave much of a gap between the mention in the newspaper and the dinner. Too much time to change their minds or figure out Edwards is a spy."

* * *

FEBRUARY 22, 1820
Grapes Tavern, Narrow Street

EDWARDS RAISED a hand as Walters entered the tavern. He ordered a bumper from the barmaid, then took a seat across from Edwards.

"I believe we're set," the spy said. "You were right. Things got a bit out of hand, but when I came up with the blunt for the weapons tomorrow, they seemed to accept the plot. Thistlewood is at sixes and sevens. Thinks he's starting a new world. He'll be a hero, and all the common folk will stand up behind him and overthrow the Crown."

"*And* he'll be in charge, I suppose."

"Aye."

"I'll be with the Runners across the street at the public house. If things go awry, look for me. I'll get you out safe." Walters took a pull of his ale. "Let me know if there are any changes."

The two men shook hands, and Walters left. He took the same route he always did and wasn't surprised to see Roger Lynch stroll up next to him.

"Dangerous neighborhood, Mr. Walters. It ain't safe to be walking about on your own," the lad said with a grin. His black curls pushed out from beneath his cap.

"I appreciate it, Mr. Lynch."

"Aw, Roger is good enough." The young man stuck his hands in his pockets as he walked. "Ma wanted me to give ye this."

Walters squinted at the proffered gift. A white linen handkerchief with his initials embroidered on it. A lump formed in his throat. "Tell her thank you." He folded it carefully and tucked it inside the pocket of his coat.

"We bought the best we could afford, and she did the needlework. Says she's happy to keep up the darning for Mrs. O'Brien. And anything else ye might need." He squinted up at the sliver of moon. "It was good o' ye to provide the meal at Christmastide and the gifts for the li'l ones. Ma found out they didn't come from the church."

Walters grew uncomfortable under the praise. He'd done so little. "The new place is working out, then?"

"Three rooms, Mr. Walters. *Three*," he crooned. "A kitchen

big enough for a table and a couple of rockers by the hearth, and two smaller rooms. One for Ma and me sister, one for me and my little brother."

"Roger," Walters said, an idea forming, "I need you to do something for me tomorrow."

CHAPTER 19

February 23, 1820
Cato Street near Grosvenor Square

𝒲 alters sat with Richard Burnie, the Bow Street magistrate, and twelve other Runners. Waiting. And waiting. The Coldstream Guards were supposed to join them, and they would surround and enter the Cato Street base together. The radicals' meeting place, a loft above a livery, was down the street from The Horse and Groom, a public house where Walters and the men presently twiddled their thumbs.

Surprise was key to avoiding any violence. With the premises so public, the magistrate didn't want any innocent bystanders hurt.

Walters had set Roger Lynch near Lord Harrowby's home early this morning. The Spencean who had worked for the Lord President of the Council had indeed paid a visit. Walters had sent word to Edwards in case the staff had said there was no dinner that day. He'd instructed Edwards to say the servants had been lying, and the news of the cabinet meeting had accidentally been published.

Walters had breathed a sigh of relief when the radicals had entered the back stairs of the livery in the midafternoon. By seven-thirty, the Bow Street magistrate called for the men to move. They couldn't wait for reinforcements any longer or the Spenceans would leave for Grosvenor Square.

"Don't try to be a hero," Walters advised Eli. His youngest brother was still a Runner, though the family knew he might take a different path than Sampson and Ben had.

"I won't," he promised, running a hand through his dark-blonde waves before replacing his hat. He turned to another Runner. "We have too much living to do yet. Right, Smithers?"

His fellow Runner laughed and shook his head. "That's why I'm second in line and not first. Besides, you still owe me a drink after this," Smithers reminded him.

"But be sure to follow your own advice, Harry." Eli gave his oldest brother an elbow. He was being overly jocular, a sure sign he was nervous. "I'll buy you a bumper, too, when we finish with this business."

The men slipped out the back of the public house. The Runners surrounded the livery, and Walters checked to see that Clayton and Gus were both at opposite ends of the street. They had been called in over an hour ago when the reinforcement had failed to arrive to apprehend any runaways.

The magistrate entered the livery first, quietly warning the men working in the stable. At his signal, the rest entered silently, moving single file up the stairs to the loft. The magistrate kicked the door open, and someone inside the loft yelled, "Extinguish the light!"

There was a pause in the line, and Walters cursed,

knowing Eli was ahead of him. He could hear cries of surprise, scuffles, and a shout of pain. When he made it to the top step, he saw a Runner down. His heart stopped until he realized it wasn't Eli.

Walters heard the magistrate demand the conspirators halt. Some ran, some dropped their weapons, others refused. One of the men lunged for Edwards, a knife in his hand. "I know this is your doing, you bloody traitor."

Walters lurched forward, grabbing the assailant's wrist. They fought for control, but he was able to overpower the man. The knife clattered to the wood floor.

Within minutes, a case that had taken years of surveillance was over. Unfortunately, Thistlewood and three others had escaped by jumping out a back window. He hoped they crossed paths with Clayton and Gus. The remaining radicals were arrested.

There was no need for a physician. Eli sank to his knees next to his friend, Smithers. Walters put a hand on his brother's shoulder and squeezed. "I'm sorry."

Eli shook his head, wiping away a tear with the back of his hand. "This is why I can't follow you, Harry. I want to help the family, but I hate the violence."

Outside, Walters saw Gus walking up the street with a body slung over his shoulder. The giant grinned. "This fellow ran right into my fist. It was the strangest thing. He seemed to be in quite a hurry."

* * *

A WEEK LATER
   Gracechurch Street

. . .

WALTERS RETURNED from the Dog's Bone a wee drunk, as Paddy would say. He wasn't stumbling. His speech wasn't slurred. But he couldn't wipe the grin from his face. This was what always gave him away. Maggie told him he always looked like a green boy in April and May when he was foxed. But he had needed to celebrate. The other radicals, including Thistlewood, had been caught. Two of the Spenceans had agreed to talk to avoid hanging. The gallows would soon be crowded with traitors.

Walters made it halfway up the staircase before Paddy called him. Turning, he faced the man who he considered his father. "Why do you always wait until I'm halfway up the stairs before you call me? Why not call for me as I pass by the door?"

"Habit," Paddy said with a grin, his blue eyes twinkling. "Ye have company, Harry."

"Demmed company," he mumbled, thinking of his warm bed upstairs.

In the parlor stood the Earl of Darby and Lord Chester Hatford. Walters paused, then removed his hat. "G'evening," he said with a nod to the men. "To what do I owe the pleasure?"

Paddy handed him a whisky. "Sit, boyo."

Unease swished in his belly. He sat on the chaise longue, joined by Paddy and his wolfhound, lying on his master's feet. The guests took the chairs, drinks already in hand.

"I've come upon some interesting information you seem to have forgotten to pass on," said Darby quietly.

Walters blinked. He recognized the earl's quiet but lethal tone. *Mattie.* His heart pounded; his palms began to sweat. Would she be punished? Had he tarnished the name of the O'Brien Investigative Services?

"My fiancée has informed me that my sister has feelings for you. And she met with you many times, without my permission, and then you jilted her." Darby crossed his legs and leaned back in the chair, his dark-blue eyes never leaving Walters's face.

Rage roared in his chest. He stood, fists clenched. Aonarach rose to face the guests, mane bristling in support of Walters. "That's not true. She said she told you of the commoner she was meeting. I helped her practice speaking with men—for this Season—so she would be more comfortable and not stumble while conversing."

Darby's eyes widened. "You were the working man?"

Walters nodded, and Paddy pulled him back to his seat, the dog following suit. "Easy, Son."

"So it was not only Miss Pendleton who helped her master the shyness." Darby pursed his lips. "Why didn't you tell me?"

"She asked me not to. I tried to tell her no—several times —but when those doe eyes are pleading with you... How could I deny her?"

Darby snorted. "*That* I understand. Did you know how she felt?"

Walters nodded. "What did she tell you?"

"Nothing. I've had an earful from my fiancée."

"And I've had an earful from mine," added Lord Chester.

"I beg your pardon?" Walters was confused. "Your fiancée?"

"The inimitable Lady Roberta." Hatford grinned. "But that's a story for another time and a decanter or two of brandy."

"My lords, I can only say I am truly sorry. I am not a man of great emotions, and Lady Matilda took me by surprise." He let out a loud huff. "I should have informed you, Lord Darby. Please do not let my actions reflect on our family business. I take full responsibility."

"Good to hear. Why did you stop the... encounters? And are you still lurking around my mews at night?"

The devil. "I wasn't lurking. I was surveilling. And I had no choice but to end it. I'm an orphan from the rookery. I live in Cheapside. She is..." He scrubbed his face with one hand. "A diamond of the first water. A kind, intelligent, and beautiful woman who deserves the best in life. *An earl's sister.*"

"Ah, there's the rub," agreed Darby. He sighed. "If the world was different, if you had been born to a noble family, would you pursue her?"

"Until my last breath." Hope surged in his chest. These were good men, peers with integrity. They might overlook this dalliance and not let it shine a poor light on the Peelers.

Lord Chester and Darby exchanged looks, then smiled at Walters. "Hatford and I are recommending you for a knighthood. The Crown is grateful for your work and the risk you took. You saved the life of Edwards and helped to stop a plot against His Majesty's government."

Walters sat like a stone, stunned. "A what? I was only doing my job."

Darby chuckled. "It is just that attitude which makes Hatford want you to have the knighthood. My reason is a bit more selfish."

"My lord?" The ale was out of his system. He was sober as a stone, and his gut told him something important was about to happen.

"My sister has been miserable. I hear her cry at night sometimes as I pass her chamber door. It breaks my heart." Darby rolled his eyes. "And Miss Pendleton's. If Mattie is not happy, none of us will be."

"What he's trying to say, Walters, is you will be Sir Harry." He blinked. *Sir Harry Walters?*

"Now ye've got him bewildered, Darby." Paddy punched

Harry's arm. "Ye can't make a silk purse out o' a sow's ear, eh?"

Walters swallowed back the chuckle rising in his throat, but it grew into a full laugh, then a guffaw. Paddy joined him, then Darby and Hatford, until they were all bellowing and holding their stomachs.

Paddy wiped a tear from his eye. "There are times when the castle ye build in the sky can be pulled down to earth. Are ye strong enough to do that, boyo?"

"But it's not a *real* title. Is it?" For the first time since he met Lady Matilda, his heart swelled with hope.

Darby nodded. "You'll need fortitude to withstand my mother's comments and demeanor. She won't be happy. But my sister will be Lady Walters *and* happy, so I am satisfied."

Walters jumped up and held out his hand. "Thank you, my lord." He shook Lord Chester's hand. "And thank you."

"I have one request," Darby added.

Walters froze. Had it been a trick? Maybe he was dreaming, and the stipulation would be the thing to wake him.

"I'd like the courtship to last a year. I know it's a long wait, but I want to be sure my sister is happy. If she is only smitten, we'll know after a year. If you are both still willing next December, I will have the banns read." Darby raised a golden brow, waiting for an answer.

Walters grinned. "I'm known for my patience, my lord. It's your sister who will be cross as a bag of weasels."

CHAPTER 20

The next day
Berkeley Square

"You have a visitor, Lady Matilda," the butler informed her from the doorway of the library. "Are you at home?"

Mattie sighed. It was most likely Lord Smalley. She really would rather finish the book, but that would be rude. And unkind. "Tell Lord Smalley I will see him in the drawing room."

Mr. Hamley cleared his throat, the top of his bald head red. She hid a smile.

"Yes?"

"I have already placed him there but... he is not Lord Smalley."

"Oh?" This did pique her interest. She set down the book and rose, intent on meeting the guest. "Who is it?"

"A Mr. Walters."

She froze. Her heart stopped. Then it began again, thumping in her chest so she couldn't hear anything but the loud beat. *Ba-bump, ba-bump*. Why would he be *calling on* her —here? Did he bring bad news? Had something happened to Nicholas?

Mattie picked up her skirts and ran down the stairs, bursting into the drawing room. Her chest heaved, and she ran to him, grabbed his coat lapels with her fist. She was terrified, for only something monumental would bring him here so openly.

"What's happened to Nicky?" Her voice sounded shrill and panicked. She tried to draw in a deep breath and calm her racing pulse.

Mr. Walters stared down at her, a smile on his face. "Lord Darby was well when I spoke with him yesterday."

Her lungs deflated, and she collapsed onto a chair. When she'd caught her breath, she glared up at him. "I think you took ten years off my life with such a fright. Why are you here, Mr. Walters?"

"Harry."

"Yes... *Harry*... why are you here?" She took in his features now. It had been so long since she'd seen him this close. Her fingers reached up to trace the streaks of gray at his temples before she buried her hands firmly in her lap. He was so handsome, but there were circles beneath his eyes, telling her he hadn't slept.

"I certainly don't want you to age ten years when our life together hasn't begun." Harry went down on his knees, face-to-face with her. His dark-brown eyes shone with love. She blinked back hot tears.

Our life together hasn't begun.

As in, it would begin?

"Excuse me? Our what?"

"Lady Matilda Bancroft, I am a simple man with a full

heart. I promise to love you and cherish you until the day I die." He took one of her hands and kissed the palm. "Your life will not be as luxurious as you are accustomed to, but you will never want for anything."

Hot tears sprang to Mattie's eyes. Was he proposing? This man who'd stolen her heart when he'd saved a boy and was attacked by mute swans? She waited. She held her breath. She looked him straight in his beautiful, honest eyes.

"Will you marry me and give me a piece of heaven while I'm still on this earth?"

"Yes!" she cried and threw herself at him. He caught her and tumbled backwards, holding her atop him.

Mattie kissed him, not caring who walked in or what anyone thought. She kissed him with all the love in her heart, with all the frustration she'd kept locked away these past months, with all the happiness of a girl who had always longed for love but never dared to hope for it.

Then she put her elbows on his chest. "How did this come about? Have you spoken with my brother?"

Harry nodded. "But it wouldn't be prudent for him to see us like—"

"I assume the lady said yes?" Darby asked from the doorway.

Mattie looked up at her brother from the floor. "Yes. How did you know about... him? Why are you approving of a union between us?" She looked to Harry, then back to Nicholas. Men were impossible to understand.

"If you sit in a chair as Mama taught you, we will explain."

When Harry tried to sit in a chair, she pulled him next to her on the chaise longue. He took her hand in his while her brother told of Hannah and Lady Roberta's scoldings, Lady Roberta's idea to have Harry knighted, and then the stipulation of a year's courtship.

"Will you cross me on this last bit?" Darby asked.

"I could wait two years if it meant being with Harry," she said, looking into his eyes, though she answered her brother. "Knowing we will be together, and he loves me, yes. I am happy to accept those terms."

"Well, that went much easier than I thought." Nicholas rose. "I'll leave you two alone for now. Mother will be home soon. I suggest we keep this quiet until Walters is officially knighted. Then I will gently break it to her."

This time Mattie threw her arms around her brother. "I love you so, Nicky. We shall both be deliriously happy!"

* * *

ONE WEEK LATER

Mattie checked her appearance once more. She was to meet the O'Briens today. Harry assured her that they would embrace her into their fold without issue. She had her doubts. Her own mother hadn't been easily persuaded when she'd found out about the betrothal.

She wasn't worried the O'Briens would *dislike* her. It was whether they thought her the right match for Harry. She knew from the way he spoke of his family how close they were, how protective of each other. How much influence would they have over him?

Her blue wool skirts, with a midnight shade for the bodice, had a delicate border of light-rose stars embroidered on the hem and sleeves. Her square neckline was modest, and a pink topaz pendant hung around her neck with matching earbobs. Her hair was twisted loosely on her head, curls falling about her neck and cheeks. A midnight-blue silk ribbon intertwined with her blonde tresses.

She pulled on her gloves and picked up the Egyptian brown reticule, the color matching her cape. She was as ready as she would ever be.

Mr. Jones had pulled the carriage to the front. He jumped from the driver's seat, his greatcoat billowing behind him in the wind. It had begun to snow. She pulled up her hood, musing it would be a late spring.

"There you are, milady," Jones said as he helped her onto the plush bench. He had placed a heated brick on the floor so her feet would stay warm. "I heard congratulations are in order."

"How did you know?" she asked. It was true about gossip spreading like the London fog.

"When a servant sees Mr. Walters coming up to the front door and being ushered to the drawing room... It doesn't take a genius. We'll keep it on the low, ma'am. Ain't nobody's business but the two of you." He gave her a bow and tipped his hat, then climbed back up to direct the matching pair of grays.

She gazed out the window as they passed from Hanover Square to Berkeley Square, stopping to pick up Hannah. The girls had decided they would go together, instead of Mattie bringing Franny to the dinner, since Harry would be Hannah's brother-in-law in time. One big happy family. Oh, how she prayed for it. The girls chatted about the upcoming wedding until they reached Cheapside Street. Turning right on Gracechurch Street, the carriage stopped in front of a three-story brick townhouse with a black-iron fence surrounding it. It had a wide portico with large windows on each side.

Mr. Jones pulled down the steps and helped the ladies from the coach. Above the double-wide front doors was a brass horseshoe pointing up, with a figure nested in the bottom of it. As they ascended the steps, Mattie saw two crossed pistols with a creature set in the center. "What is that?" she asked Hannah. It looked like a lion with a hawk's head and wings.

"It's a griffin, milady," offered Mr. Jones. "An ancient Celtic symbol."

The door opened, not by a butler but by Mr. Walters himself. "Ladies, welcome!"

She entered the short receiving hall, with light paneling on the walls and a gas light above. There was a door on the left, and the parlor on the right, where a crowd of people were talking loudly. It *looked* like a crowd compared to her household. Mattie grabbed Hannah's hand.

"Oh, such a big family," her friend exclaimed, except her voice was full of excitement instead of nerves or dread. "And they will soon be ours."

"They look much more intimidating than they really are," Harry whisper-shouted. "Especially the big blunderhead with the dark hair and paws like a bear."

"Are you talking about me?" bellowed Gus. "Don't disparage me in front of my future sister-in-law."

"Ye or da dog. His description fit da both o' ye," Paddy said with a laugh.

Nora hurried into the hall, her copper curls unbound. "I'm Nora, and please ignore my beetle-headed brothers," she said, hugging both girls. "I'm so happy to see you again, *Sister*. This must be Miss Pendleton."

"You look familiar," said Hannah, tapping her lower lip with a finger. "I never forget a face."

"She was the concubine at the masquerade," Harry explained.

Hannah paled at the mention of the masquerade but soon rallied. "Oh my, the whole family is in the spy business."

"Investigative service," corrected Mattie.

Nora took their cloaks, shaking off the snow, and hung them at the end of the hall. They entered the parlor, and a sea of bodies moved toward them. Mr. and Mrs. O'Brien were introduced first, both greeting her with heavy Irish accents.

He was a towering man, well over six feet with fading red hair and dark-blue eyes that sparkled with mischief. His wife was Mattie's height, matronly, with auburn hair streaked with gray and soft, kind brown eyes. She also hugged the girls. The couple made her feel at home, and the tension in her shoulders began to relax.

Then they were introduced to the second oldest, Gus the giant, his straight brown hair pulled back in a queue and intelligent dark-brown eyes assessing her. When he smiled, seeming to approve of what he saw, Mattie knew they would be good friends.

Next was Sampson, a physician with deep dimples, whose quiet voice seemed out of place in the cacophony. Clayton, an attractive man with auburn hair and deep-green eyes, was also a detective. Benjamin was the family's solicitor and legal advisor for the business. And finally Eli, the youngest male, presently finishing time as a Runner before joining the others. And Harry had been right. Mr. O'Brien's hound reached the man's hip when in a sitting position. It would easily surpass a man's height when on two legs.

The evening went quickly. The meal was excellent. A tasty leek soup was served, followed by roast goose, parsnips and potatoes, and a coarse dark bread that was delicious smothered in butter. Soda bread, Harry had called it.

Mattie was in awe of Mrs. O'Brien, who had cooked the entire meal herself. "Except for da lemon tarts. Our day girl bakes 'em better, and I won't even try to compete."

When dessert was served, the lemon tarts were just the right balance of sweet and sour with a rich, buttery crust. Hannah remarked on the horseshoe over the door.

"What is the lion-bird figure sitting in the horseshoe?"

"A griffin. It's a Celtic symbol representing loyalty and strength," explained Paddy.

"Light over darkness, goodness over evil," added Harry.

"It's what we fight for every day. Those pistols beneath were added when Paddy began the Peelers."

After dinner, resuming their place in the parlor, the music began. This was a group who spent much time as a family, seen in the way they sang or danced together, finished one another's sentences, and laughed at private jokes from their childhoods. They were quick to share embarrassing stories of one another growing up, and Mattie hadn't laughed so hard since… she was a child.

They were the type of family she had always been both envious and terrified of. But the fear had receded, replaced with a feeling of belonging. Before the end of the evening, she had been teased, defended, and teased again. They asked so many unexpected questions that she thought her head would spin. But never once did she feel unwanted or judged.

"You realize, coming from a small family myself, you'll have to share them," Hannah whispered in her ear as Madeira was passed around.

Mr. and Mrs. O'Brien took the wingback chairs by the hearth and signaled to Nora. "Honora plays a digestive melody after dinner, so our stomachs settle before the games begin," explained the matriarch.

Later, Mattie asked the question still on her mind. "How did this family come about?"

"Oh, yes," Hannah chimed in, "tell us, please."

CHAPTER 21

*T*he O'Briens looked at each other, and Maggie nodded.

"I was a constable in Dublin. T'ings were getting hostile in the city, and da force was poorly paid and overworked. There was no organization, and I was getting frustrated. Maggie's half brother was English and wrote to us about da Bow Street Runners and da work dey were doing in London."

"It must have been hard to move so far from family," sympathized Hannah.

"He spoke for me, and I became a Runner. Our basket was full, and we were happy."

Maggie cut in, "Our basket was fine, but it was not full. I could not bear a child and was in a dreadful state. One day, Paddy comes in da door, carrying a skinny lad burning up with fever." They both cast a loving gaze on Harry. "An orphan who'd been sold to... Anyway, he'd been cast out when he fell ill."

"I came upon a group of boys, beating mercilessly on a wee lad. He was holding something in his coat and putting up a fierce fight. I disposed of da hooligans, picked da lad up, and brought him home," finished Mr. O'Brien, reaching down to rub his dog's head.

"And our family began."

"What were you so determined to keep?" Mattie asked Harry.

"A box my mother had left with me. The name *Walters* had been carved on the lid, and somehow, I always knew it was my father's name."

"Next was Gus. He was sold to a chimney sweep," Paddy continued. "Da man was beating da boy because he'd grown so fast in two months dat he couldn't do his job. I paid da scalawag a good price and took da boy myself."

"Best day of my life," said Gus with a sappy smile. "Only the good Lord knows what might have happened to me if this big burly angel hadn't come along at the exact time he did."

Dr. Brooks's soft voice entered the conversation. "My father was swindled with a fraudulent insurance policy. When our bookstore burned, we were ruined. They were sent to debtor's prison, and I tried to earn money on the street to get them out. Or at least feed them. Being an academic, you can imagine I didn't do well."

"He tried to pick my pocket," Paddy said, slapping his knee. "But I saw da intelligence and da desperation in his eyes. He was number t'ree. Liked scientific things—plants, healing herbs—wanted to be a doctor."

"My mother, a friend of Maggie's, died of a fever. She took me in without blinking an eye," said Clayton. "She's been a second mother to me, and Paddy the only father I've known."

They moved on to Benjamin and Elijah, each man helping with the telling of his story. Ben had a desire to learn the law, after seeing so many, including his own family, unjustly punished. The O'Briens educated him and sent him to the Inns of Court. He now represented the Peelers, gave legal advice, and helped them prepare the cases which needed to go to a barrister and be heard in court.

Eli was an old soul who had a talent for sketching. Now finishing his second year as a Peeler, Eli had decided not to be an investigator. He was no coward, but he could not tolerate a lifetime of the violence that Runners and Peelers must endure.

Maggie cast an affectionate look at her youngest son. "Ye'll find yer way, won't ye, my sweet boy?"

Eli's neck turned red at the endearment. "Yes, ma'am. But my future will always be tied to our family in some way."

"They saved the best for last," piped Nora with a grin.

"Aye, our only girl." Maggie beamed. "She was left as a bairn on the steps of da hospital. A friend who worked in the children's ward saw her mop of red hair and knew she was an O'Brien. Since we had no idea where she came from, she was given our surname."

Paddy sighed. "One look at the wee child, and she stole our hearts."

"I've been doted on and raised by six brothers besides my parents," said Nora. "It's no wonder I can throw a knife and shoot a pistol as well as most men, then toss a dress over my head and woo them until I get my way."

"Which she always does," added Gus, sending everyone into laughter.

It was obvious these adults, raised by the childless Irish couple, were devoted to each other. Mattie saw the love on each face and knew they would all give their lives for the other. She blinked back the unexpected tears. "Your family is more loyal and loving than many who share the same blood."

"It is a testament to you both, Mr. and Mrs. O'Brien, on

your skills as parents and the warmth of your affection," added Hannah.

When Mattie asked about sending for Mr. Jones, Harry insisted he take the ladies home. Mattie was secretly thrilled. They could take Hannah home, and she would have a few minutes alone with him.

* * *

HARRY HAD ALREADY ARRANGED for Roger to be ready to drive the carriage that evening. The lad had arrived after dinner and waited in the kitchen, enjoying a good meal, until it was time to fetch the carriage.

Seeing the lad in a fine greatcoat, the top hat on the table next to Roger's empty plate, made Harry smile. Fate had sent him past that alley the night he'd found the boy.

They took Hannah home, who promised to call on Mattie the next day. Harry knocked on the roof of the carriage, then poked his head out the window. "Mr. Lynch, park at Hanover Square before you take us to the townhouse."

"Yes, Mr. Walters," the driver called back.

"He seems young," Mattie said as Harry leaned back against the squabs.

"He's just sixteen, but he grew into manhood early. I stumbled upon him near the docks when a gang of cloak twitchers tried to rob him."

"Following in the O'Briens' footsteps and collecting your own waifs?"

He shrugged, embarrassed. "*We* offered him a job. Whatever he makes of himself from there is his own doing."

"Your tough exterior hides such a massive heart." She kissed his cheek.

Just the mere whisper of a touch sent desire rumbling through his body. He cupped her cheek with one hand, tipped his head, and brushed her lips with his. A whimper bubbled in her throat, making him smile against her mouth.

"This will be the longest year of my life," he murmured, his forehead touching hers. "But you are worth every moment of torture."

"Is it too long to wait?" she asked as her fingers played with his cravat.

He shook his head and leaned back against the squabs again, pulling her next to him and kissing the top of her head. The carriage had come to a stop. "No, I think your brother is wise to have us wait."

"Why?" She looked up at him, concern in her eyes. "In case you change your mind?"

Harry laughed. "No, love, in case you do."

She opened her mouth to argue, and he laid a finger over her lips.

"You are young, ten years my junior, and I assume I am your first romantic encounter with a man."

Her silence told him it was true. "If your love is misguided, wrapped up in a feeling of gratitude or appreciation for my help, or if you find you were only smitten—as a young woman could easily be—you will have the opportunity to change your mind."

Her lips trembled as if he'd hurt her. "You must understand, Mattie. I want—no, I need—you to be happy for a lifetime. If you ever regretted for a moment your decision to marry me, that regret would break my heart even more than living without you." He tipped her chin up with his thumb and kissed her eyes, then her nose, and finally her sweet, sweet lips. "You deserve the best in life, and I don't mean material things. I mean the contentment of a well-matched marriage, the bliss of a family, the ecstasy of love."

* * *

MATTIE LEANED INTO HIS KISS, her heart full. Silly man, thinking she'd ever change her mind. He didn't know her as well as he thought. But the *not* knowing was part of the courtship. Learning one another's likes and dislikes, moods, facial expressions, which touch made his eyes go dark with desire or her breath come in pants, what made the other laugh.

"I read somewhere that love is a journey, full of surprises and joy, unexpected moments of pain and sadness. But always, it is a journey to be experienced and savored." She paused, searching for the right words. "But the foundation of our love is solid. The storms we encounter may rock us, but we will always remain upright, like the old towers you come across still standing in the countryside, though weathered with age."

Harry chuckled. "I'll be the old tower, and you will be the beautiful new addition the next owners add."

She did not laugh. She had to make *him* understand her love wasn't an accident or a misunderstanding. "I admit you are the reason I have bloomed, the reason I am embracing life in a new way. I always thought I could be content as a spinster rather than endure a loveless marriage. There would be other distractions to fill my life."

"Spinsterhood would be the worst fate for you, sweetheart."

"When you came along, I saw the world had so much more to offer and how much I had hidden away from it. I used my books as an excuse and an escape, for reading the pages was much safer than experiencing it firsthand. But the most vital thing you gave me was the realization that I didn't want to be alone.

"Even without you, I could be happy, better off than if I'd never known you. I need *you* to realize how you showed me there are choices. *I* have choices. And I choose you."

He looked straight ahead, his expression unreadable in the shadows. She touched his cheek and turned his face to her. "There is something else. What is it, Harry?"

"Did it shock you when they told you of my... rough beginnings? My first eight years were spent in an orphanage and then a brothel." His voice was rough, hoarse, as if the words had been forced. "I shared only bits and pieces of my past with you until tonight."

Mattie shook her head, hoping he read the love in her eyes. "Everything you've been through, everything you've experienced in your lifetime, has made you the man you are today. The man I am in love with. You brought me to life, Harry. I am the person I knew I could be—wanted to be—because of you."

He kissed her then, and the same thrumming rushed through her core as before, but something was different. This kiss was more... confident. She had eased his mind and, in doing so, eased her own.

They were a good team. Their differences would make them stronger, complementing one another as they moved through this life together. Always together.

All thanks to a petulant pair of mute swans.

THE VICAR

FEBRUARY 23, 1820

"I-I'm sorry, sir. But they been arrested. Well, most of 'em. And one Runner dead." Robert Dunn twisted his hat in his hands as he spoke to the back of the man's head. Two brawny bodyguards flanked the huge oak desk. He watched a curl of smoke twist and rise to the rafters, disappearing. Like he wanted to do.

"Who got away?" A quiet, cold voice.

It put a chill right down Dunn's spine. Rumor had it the man was disfigured. The reason no one saw his face. Robert couldn't wait to get home to his wife. Dottie would have a hot supper and a smile waiting. *If* he got home. "Thistlewood, but they'll find him soon enough."

"They haven't found you."

"True 'nough." Dunn shuffled his feet. He was a proud man, full of himself, so people said. But The Vicar put a knot in his belly. Of course, a knot in his belly was better than a knotted noose around his neck. "I was born in London, know these streets and alleys better'n most."

"This was a scheme dear to my heart," The Vicar said. "I'm disappointed, and that's not a good thing for anyone."

AUBREY WYNNE

Dunn nodded his head, then realized his boss couldn't see it. "Yessir. What do you want me to do?"

"Stay down for a few months. You should have enough to get by. Don't try to make some blunt on the side and get caught. Newgate will be the least of your worries."

Dunn swallowed. Sweat trickled down his back. "Yessir. I'll wait for word."

"You do that."

Dunn walked to the door.

"Oh, and Mr. Dunn?"

"Yessir?"

"Don't disappoint me again."

EPILOGUE

September 1821

$\mathcal{M}$attie stepped from the carriage, her hand in Harry's as they returned to the same spot in St. James's Park where they had first met. He carried a basket with lunch and a blanket slung over his arm. She held a parasol above their heads, twirling it and pretending to protect them from the bright sun.

"Please tell me the location is the only part of this anniversary we are recreating. I do not relish getting near the swans," Harry said as he spread the blanket.

"No, you ninnyhammer." She sat down and tucked her legs beneath her. Their townhouse was close to the park, just off Haymarket near St. James's Square. They were on the outskirts of the wealthier neighborhoods, but theirs was very acceptable and well-to-do. Appropriate for the salary Harry made, and suitable enough for any friends of a higher station to visit.

Mattie had been surprised at how quickly their year of courtship had passed. They were married the following February, after securing the home they now shared. Harry had refused any financial help from Nicholas. Though her brother had insisted on buying them a carriage and a matching pair of horses as a wedding gift.

"Your mother smiled at me last week when we visited the baby," Harry mused as he studied the clouds passing above them. "I think it may be the first voluntary and *sincere* smile since we've met."

"She said you are growing on her," Mattie told him.

"Like a moss on a stone?"

She laughed. "It doesn't matter. Mama is finally accepting you, as we all knew she would."

"Are you happy?" he asked out of the blue. "Is there anything I could do to make you happier?"

Mattie shook her head. Marriage was everything she had hoped for. Her hand went to her belly, remembering their passionate morning together and the babe growing inside her.

"Look," she said, pointing at the pond. "Another family of swans."

"Don't attract their attention, please. I still carry a scar from the last encounter."

"Well, I understand their protectiveness. I only hope I'm not quite as waspish with our baby." An impish grin turned up her mouth. "Though perhaps with this first one…"

"When we have—" Harry gave her a side-glance and read her face. "Our first one?"

She nodded.

"You're with child?" he whispered.

She nodded again. "Papa Walters."

He jumped up and pulled her to him, giving her a lusty

kiss in front of God and whoever else passed by. He waved to a couple staring at them.

"I'm going to be a father!"

The couple nodded in understanding, smiling and waving back as they continued their walk.

He put his head back and yelled to the sky, "We're having a baby!"

But when their eyes met again, there was panic darkening his brown gaze. "What if I'm a terrible father?"

Mattie laughed, her shoulders shaking. Her orphaned husband already played benefactor to Roger's brother and sister. "You've become a wonderful father-figure to Mr. Lynch. *And* his siblings. You will be a wonderful papa, *Sir Harry*."

"Only because I married the best woman in London. No, in all of England, *Lady Walters*."

"Shall we tell my family first or yours?" Mattie took a deep breath, thinking of the chaotic O'Brien household when they announced their news. Both Sampson and Clayton were married now, but Harry would give the family the first grandchild.

Life was full of promise and hope and love and family. The years ahead fanned out like a welcoming parade. And the shy girl who had first met her heart's desire here, in this park, was now the master of the parade.

REVIEWS ARE the life blood of any author. If you enjoyed this story, please consider leaving a few words of review at your favorite retailer.

If you'd like to join my mailing list to keep up on future releases, sales, and contests:

AUTHOR'S NOTE

I love mixing fiction with historical persons, places, and events. The streets of Cheapside and other parts of London are real. I have two giant maps on my office wall with colored markers showing crime scenes, character addresses, and meeting places. My husband says I'm only a few sticky notes away from "A Beautiful Mind." I hope he's wrong. 😄 The Peterloo Massacre mentioned below was also part of *Rhapsody and Rebellion* (Once Upon a Widow series) and the MacNaughton series, *Deception and Desire* and *An Allusive Love*.

The Grapes, Limehouse

One of the taverns Harry frequents for his investigations is The Grapes, Limehouse. It is a tavern with 500 years of history and is still open today. It is on the Thames, near the Canary Wharf, and it is noted that Charles Dickens was a patron there. The leaseholder of the building is Ian McKellen. I plan on visiting for their Monday night Pub Quiz on my next visit to London. Here's a link to see it for yourself. http://thegrapes.co.uk

Aonarach, the Irish wolfhound

The Irish wolfhound in this series is based on my own wolfhound, Solo. He was the only pup to survive of his litter. He overcame several major health issues, including gangrene in his tail that was docked. We received this big galoot at six months because he was pet quality and not eligible for the show ring. We didn't care. The name Aonarach (Ay-nuh-rok) means "only" in Irish Gaelic.

The Cato Street Conspiracy

The radical Arthur Thistlewood was a real villain. He joined the Spencean Philanthropists in 1811. By 1816, he was considered a "dangerous character" by police spies. After the Peterloo Massacre earlier that year (a massive assembly of people peacefully protesting), unrest in the country increased. The Spenceans arranged a mass meeting at Spa Fields, Islington, for the orator Henry Hunt (who also spoke at the fatal Peterloo Massacre). Over 300,000 attended.

The plan was to encourage rioting in London, so they could seize the reins of government by occupying the Tower of London and Bank of England. It failed, one man was stabbed, and the radicals were arrested. However, the spy sent in by the Home Office also had a criminal record and declared an unreliable witness. The radicals were released. Thistlewood's aggressive strategies was too much for their leader, James Watson. Arthur took over.

Their next plot (in our story) was to eliminate the government ministers. Another spy, George Edwards (also a real person in this story), infiltrated the Spencean Philanthropists. They met frequently, renting a hayloft above a livery on Cato Street. The location was very close to 39 Grosvenor Square where Lord Harrowby resided and still stands today. Edwards, not trusted by most of the members, was able to convince Thistlewood of his loyalty. He showed the group an article in t, reporting the Cabinet would meet at Harrowby's on February 23. Suggesting they murder the members while they ate, he also provided the funds needed to purchase the weapons for the assassinations.

One of the members, William Davidson, had worked for the earl and checked with staff that morning. When he relayed to Thistlewood there was no dinner, and the earl was out of town, the Spencean leader became adamant the servants were lying. They continued as planned, gathering their weapons (mostly pistols and grenades) and meeting at the Cato Street loft. Across the street, the Bow Street magistrate, Richard Birnie, waited in a public house. When the Coldstream Guard didn't show (turns out they were waiting at the wrong end of the street), they entered the house at 7:30. One Runner was killed by Thistlewood, a sword in his gut, and the rest were arrested or escaped. Thistlewood and three others escaped but were quickly picked up. The murdered man, Richard Smithers, was also an actual person.

On April 28, most of the accused were sentenced to be hanged, drawn, and quartered for high treason, later reduced to only hanging. Robert Adams and John Monument gave evidence and testified to avoid charges. The sentences of Charles Cooper, Richard Bradburn, John Harrison, James Wilson, and John Strange were commuted to transportation for life.

On May 1, 1820, Arthur Thistlewood, Richard Tidd, James Ings, William Davidson, and John Brunt were hanged at Newgate Prison. Thousands showed up to watch the spectacle. Residents who had windows overlooking the scaffold sold seats for three guineas. The crowd remained peaceable, booing and hissing after the men were cut down and their heads removed, placed in a coffin along with the body.

Quotes from observers:

George Theodore Wilkinson described Thistlewood being interviewed after his arrest in May, 1820.

"My genius is so great just now, I don't think there is any man

alive has so great a genius as mine at the moment." Then he would pour upon the ground for a minute or two in deep cogitation; and at length break into the following soliloquy: "If it is the will of the Author of the World that I should perish in the cause of freedom - his will, and not mine, be done! It would be quite a triumph to me!" - at the same time throwing his arms about in a manner which savoured strongly of insanity.

Quote from an observer

John Hobhouse, a government minister, observed the executions and that night wrote about it in his diary (1st May, 1820)

The men died like heroes. Ings, perhaps, was too obstreperous in singing 'Death or Liberty', and Thistlewood said, "Be quiet, Ings; we can die without all this noise."

If you'd like to know more about this conspiracy and see the livery where it happened, follow this link: https://www.youtube.com/watch?v=E8rlmnFiMbs

ABOUT THE AUTHOR

USA Today Bestselling author Aubrey Wynne resides in the Midwest with her husband, dogs, horses, mule, and barn cats. Obsessions include wine, history, travel, trail riding, and all things Christmas. Her Chicago Christmas series and historical romances have received multiple awards and nominations as a Rone finalist by InD'tale Magazine.

Aubrey's first love is medieval romance but after dipping her toe in the Regency period in 2018 with the *Wicked Earls' Club*, she was smitten. This inspired her sweet Regency spin-off series *Once Upon a Widow*, and a steamy Scottish Regency series, *A MacNaughton Castle Romance*. Her Regency detective series, *Paddy's Peelers*, will launch in 2025.

Social Media Links:
Website:
http://www.aubreywynne.com
Facebook:
https://www.facebook.com/magnificentvalor
Aubrey's Ever After Facebook group:
https://www.facebook.com/groups/
AubreyWynnesEverAfters/
Twitter:
https://twitter.com/Aubreywynne51
Pinterest:
https://www.pinterest.com/aubreywynne51/

Instagram:
https://www.instagram.com/Aubreywynne51
Bookbub page:
https://www.bookbub.com/profile/aubrey-wynne
<u>Goodreads:</u>
https://www.goodreads.com/author/show/7383937.
Aubrey_Wynne

Sign up for my newsletter and don't miss future releases
https://www.subscribepage.com/k3f1z5

ALSO BY AUBREY WYNNE

ONCE UPON A WIDOW©

Once Upon a Widow series

Earl of Sunderland #1

Maggie award, International Digital Awards finalist

Christopher Roker inherited the title of rake. She hides behind her independence. Fate accepts the challenge...

Escaping his late brother's memory, Lady Grace is a welcome distraction. But as the attraction grows, Kit finds himself wavering between his old military life and the lure of an exceptional but unwilling woman.

A Wicked Earl's Widow #2

Recommended by InD'tale Magazine

Eliza, Lady Sunderland, is widowed after one year. Her abusive father, near financial ruin, is already planning another wedding.

When Viscount Pendleton discovers a beauty defending an elderly woman against ruffians, he is smitten. But Nate soon realizes he must discover Eliza's dark past to save the woman he loves.

Rhapsody and Rebellion #3

Maggie finalist, nominated for Rone Award, InD'tale Magazine

A Scottish legacy... A political rebellion... Two hearts destined to meet...

Alisabeth was betrothed from the cradle. At seventeen, she marries her best friend and finds happiness if not passion. In less than a year, a political rebellion makes her a widow. The handsome English earl arrives a month later and rouses her desire and a terrible guilt.

Crossing the border into Scotland, Gideon finds his predictable world turned upside down. Folklore, legend, and political unrest intertwine with an unexpected attraction to a feisty Highland beauty. When the earl learns of an English plot to stir the Scots into rebellion, he must choose his country or save the clan and the woman who stirs his soul.

Earl of Darby #4

Holt Medallion Winner, NTRWA Reader's Choice Award, Nominated for Rone Award, InD'tale magazine

Miss Hannah Pendleton, nursing her pride after her childhood crush falls in love with another, hurls herself into the excitement of a first season.

Since his wife's suicide on their wedding night, the Earl of Darby has carefully cultivated his rakish reputation. But when Nicholas sees a lovely newcomer being courted by the devil himself, her innocence and candor revive the chivalry buried deep in his soul.

Earl of Brecken #5

He's on the brink of ruin. She's in search of a hero.

Notorious for his seductive charm, the Earl of Brecken searches for a wealthy heiress. His choices are dismal until he meets Miss Franklin. Guileless, gorgeous and with an enormous dowry, she seems the answer to his prayers. Until his conscience makes an unexpected appearance.

Earl of Griffith #6

Sorrow and Regrets...

After eloping, a widowed Lady Helen is disillusioned with love and raising a three-year-old alone. Now she must face the music and her family.

An unexpected ray of sunshine...

Conway, Earl of Griffith is smitten at first sight with his friend's sister and adorable daughter. But can he convince the grieving and lovely widow that love is worth a second chance?

Beware A Wallflower's Wrath #7

Annis Craigg gave her heart—and innocence—away at seventeen. When Lord Robert Harding returns to Scotland fifteen years later, he's desperate to find the only woman he's ever loved. But she has secrets and an attitude.

Lies, secrets, and betrayal will challenge the fierce love of a steadfast Highlander and remorseful but determined Englishman. Will destiny find a way to bring two star-crossed souls together?

A Wallflower's Wassail Punch #8

Lady Annette's first Season was a disaster after a duke's son pinched her by the punchbowl, and she walloped him in the nose. Five years of malicious rumors later, her father offers an outrageous dowry so he too can marry.

Lord Wilkinson, a widower, meets a striking, intelligent woman, with a dry wit only he seems to appreciate. His heart stirs for the first time in decades. But will their age difference and wagging tongues interfere with their budding romance?

The Scoundrel's Christmas Challenge #9

A contest to win her fortune...

Lady Winfield, a long-time wealthy widow, is infamous for her outrageous house parties. While hosting her annual Christmastide gathering, Christiana proposes a new game: a daily challenge of her choice. She will accept the proposal of the man who can best her at three or more competitions by Twelfth Night. Though all agree to the diversion, no one expects the games to include marksmanship, archery, and fencing.

A contest to win her heart...

When Lucius, Viscount Bolingbroke presents Lady Winfield with a secret challenge, she can't resist. Will their midnight rendezvous and private contests end in certain victory for one or a dual attraction for both?

The Duplicate Duke #10

In a country far, far away...

Lady Gwendolyn Beaumaris and her brother have been known as the Downing twins since their father's death when they were eight years old. At twenty-two, Gwen and her mother have settled in Boston while her brother tries to make his fortune in the fur trade. Down to their last pennies, she must consider marriage to a wealthy middle-aged merchant.

The brass ring is so close...

Lord Wickton has worked tirelessly the past two years to bring honor back to the family name. When the viscount learns he is the heir presumptive to his great uncle's dukedom, his prayers are answered.

A comedy of errors...

When a letter arrives announcing that Gwen's brother is the new Duke of Shackerley, mother and daughter come up with a desperate plan: Gwendolyn will impersonate her brother and assume the dukedom. But when the sinfully handsome Wickton meets them at the dock, and Gwen is hopelessly smitten.

A tale of love, deception, and the power of fate will entangle a desperate viscount with a daring female. Can he forgive her charade, or will he snuff out the burning passion that rages in her heart.

Kiss the Scoundrel Farewell #11

Lady Margaret marries out of duty only to find herself in the center of a scandal. Her husband, Baron Drake, dies in a duel over another woman. With no children and no desire to be shackled again, Meg decides to enjoy life as men do. She will be the other woman instead of the wife held captive by the whims of a man. Lady Drake enjoys the freedom of her widow's status.

Simon, Lord Hayward, a dutiful son with no fantasies of love, agrees to marry a wealthy heiress to plump the family's coffers. His father, in love with his mistress for decades, sets out to find his son one of his own. Simon scoffs at the idea, but when he meets an alluring courtesan at a masquerade, he finds himself smitten.

In a twist of fate, the masks come off, and Simon and Meg realize they met years ago, sharing a kiss in a duke's garden. Their secrets come out: She is no courtesan, and he is betrothed. After the viscount confesses his love, the baroness flees for the safety of the countryside.

As Lady Drake begins to doubt her scheme of being a paramour, Lord Hayward wonders if he can be happy with a wife who is not Meg and searches her out. He seeks her out only to find danger lurking in the idyllic English hills, and they soon learn the past has consequences no matter who you pretend to be.

A Paddy's Peelers Mystery series

Set in the hectic district of Cheapside during the Regency, Paddy's Peelers search the dregs of London with skill and cunning to bring criminals to justice and, perhaps, unexpectedly find love along the way. A sweet but action-packed romance.

Crime, Conspiracies, and Courtship #1

Lady Matilda has always been an introvert, preferring her books to awkward conversations with strangers. As her first Season arrives, her mother insists she put away her bluestocking and concentrate on finding a husband. But Mattie is terrified of finding herself betrothed or even worse— not betrothed. The arrogant men of the ton terrify her.

Mr. Harry Walters is an orphaned, ex-Bow Street runner turned investigator, who makes a living by his wits. Working for Paddy O'Brien and his Peelers, often taking assignments for the Home Office, Walters is used to working closely with the beau monde. When a peer approaches him about a new assignment, Harry realizes they are both after the same man. He accepts the job but soon finds himself also protecting the earl's sister.

While working in costume at a masquerade, Walters makes a fatal mistake when he asks Lady Matilda to dance. It takes only a few stolen glances and one waltz for two unlikely souls to become hopelessly entwined. Mattie is determined to win the heart of this handsome, rugged man. Harry is just as determined to keep her safe.

Will fate find a way to bring a common man and an earl's sister a happy ever after? Or will his lack of title and dangerous life keep her at arm's length?

Pads, Purses, and Plum Pudding #2

Dr. Sampson Brooks is on a case that has nothing to do with medicine. He vows to help bring down the man who ruined his father and sent his mother to an early grave. When the villain's top henchmen are apprehended, Sam attends the hanging. While closing one chapter of his story, he unexpectedly opens another.

Dottie Brown, young and naïve, is duped by a charming swindler. A year after the wedding, she learns he's not what he pretends to be. Watching him on the gallows, she vows never to be taken in by romantic notions again. Yet fate tosses two obstacles in her path that day—a handsome physician and an abandoned child.

A chance encounter reveals one woman's secret, another man's revenge, and a love that

will change their lives forever.

Poisons, Potions, and Parasols #3

She's content with her life...

Miss Eugenia Chapelle was born on the wrong side of the blanket. After her mother was disowned and fled to London, she pretended to be the widow of a French aristocrat to draw customers as a modiste. After her mother's death, Genie continues the lie, playing the half-French designer of Madame Chapelle's and running the business with her aunt. She never expects an earl to search out his illegitimate daughter twenty-six years later.

He will rip it apart...

Mr. Clayton Pierce works for one of London's most respected investigators. He has two cases on his docket—tracking a gang of counterfeiters passing banknotes and finding a long-lost child of an earl. When he meets the beautiful and talented Miss Chapelle, his attraction for her is as strong as his obsession with solving mysteries and catching criminals.

After Genie witnesses a possible murder at Hyde Park, she becomes a key witness in his first case. Then, by a twist of fate, she also becomes linked to his second assignment. With danger lurking around every dark corner, and the past the murkiest shadow of all, Clayton learns that solving a case does not always guarantee satisfaction of a job well done. As passions flare and the stakes are raised, will his success as an investigator be his ruin in love?

A MacNaughton Castle Romance series

Highland Regencies

"Witty and sensual!"

Verified Purchase Review

"Lovely characters and complicated family conflicts. You will easily get caught up in their lives."

Goodreads Review

A Merry MacNaughton Mishap (Prequel)

Rone finalist, InD'tale Magazine, N.N. Light Book Heaven finalist

Two feuding clans, one accidental encounter, a wee bit of holiday enchantment…

When Calum MacNaughton rescues a rival clan member from an icy drowning, he is unexpectedly rewarded with the clansman's most precious possession. Now Calum has until Twelfth Night to convince her to stay.

Deception and Desire #1

Nominated for Rone award, InD'tale Magazine, N.N. Light Book Heaven award winner

Two rebellious souls… An innocent deception… One scorching catastrophe…

Fenella Franklin's talents lie in numbers and a keen business mind, not in the art of flirtation. Lachlan MacNaughton has neither the temperament nor the patience to be the next MacNaughton chief, preferring to knock heads together rather than placate bickering clansmen. Their attraction sparks a passion they cannot deny. But will an innocent deception test their newfound love?

Allusive Love #2

A woman in love... An infuriating Scot… A tantalizing chase.

Kirstine has loved Brodie MacNaughton forever, but he considers Kirsty his best friend. When he turns to her for advice, she surprises him with an unexpected kiss that sends fire through his veins. When pride, Highland politics, and tragedy collide, he realizes how precious and allusive true love can be.

A Bonny Pretender #3

She's pretending to be someone she's not…   His entire life is based on a lie…

Brigid MacNaughton becomes the perfect lady to placate her family, then falls in love with a quiet, self-possessed Englishman. Lord Raines is smitten with the beguiling and demure Scot. If he divulges his scandalous parentage, will she still fall willingly into his arms? Bonny pretender vs handsome imposter… Can love overcome a double deception?

www.ingramcontent.com/pod-product-compliance
Lightning Source LLC
Chambersburg PA
CBHW020436180626
46812CB00003B/1255